SAVAGE
NIGHTS

SAVAGE NIGHTS

Cyril Collard

THE OVERLOOK PRESS
WOODSTOCK • NEW YORK

First published in 1994 by
The Overlook Press
Lewis Hollow Road
Woodstock, New York 12498

Copyright © 1989 Flammarion
Translation copyright © 1993 William Rodarmor
Originally published in France as *Les Nuits Fauves* by Flammarion
This English edition first published in Great Britain by Quartet Books Ltd. 1993.

Library of Congress Cataloging-in-Publication Data

Collard, Cyril.
[Nuits fauves. English]
Savage nights / Cyril Collard ; translated by William Rodarmor.
p.cm.
1. Motion picture producers and directors - Fiction.
2. AIDS (disease) - Patients - Fiction. 3. Man-woman
relationships - Fiction. 4. Bisexual men - Fiction.
I. Title.
PQ2663.04622N85 1993
843'.914-dc20
93-31881
CIP

ISBN: 0-87951-534-1
First American Edition

Cyril Collard, French writer, film director and actor died of an AIDS-related illness in Paris on 5 March 1993. He was born in Paris in 1957. Collard directed a film version of his autobiographical second novel, *Savage Nights*, and also starred as the lead. The film was awarded four Césars; the announcement was made seventy-two hours after his death.

William Rodarmor's translations include *The Long Way* by Bernard Moitessier, *The Carnivorous Lamb* by Agustin Gomez-Arcos and Denis Belloc's *Neons* and *Slow Death in Paris* (Quartet Books 1991 & 1992). He is the managing editor of *California Monthly*.

Night was falling when she came in. With my lips pressed against the office's picture window, I was staring at the rue de la Pompe below. A motorcycle pulled away and I watched as the white plume of its exhaust mingled with the smog hanging over the city.

The girl closed the door and I turned to face her. She hesitated, a motorcycle helmet in her hands. My assistant spoke: 'Are you Laura?'

'Yes.'

She shook hands without glancing at him. She had turned to look towards me, beyond me, through the picture window to the dark blue sky.

The outside chill clung to her, intensified by her ride here on the motorcycle. The helmet had crushed her hair, a blend of blonde and brown. She had thick eyebrows and very light, almost yellow eyes; her calm face was disturbingly beautiful, a mass of contradictions, a borrowed mask. She was dressed in black: a black motorcycle jacket, tight jeans, boots, helmet. She wasn't very tall.

'On the phone,' my assistant said, 'were you told what this was about?'

'Sort of.'

1

'We want you to do a screen test for a music video. The director and the singer will be here soon.'

She wasn't listening to him, had picked up the jacket of Marc's record from the table, and was turning it over in her hands. They looked like the hands of a forty-year-old woman.

'Is this him?' she asked.

The assistant, who had seemed ill at ease from the moment she came in, said, 'That's him. How old are you, Laura?'

'I'm eighteen.'

He rummaged through a file of photos, found Laura's, showed it to her.

'What's that?'

'That's you. Your agent must have given it to us . . .'

'I don't have an agent.'

'But you are an actress, aren't you?'

'Sometimes.'

'You know we're shooting a video, though, don't you?'

I pulled myself away from the picture window and the blue of the night, and moved towards the warmth of the room and Laura.

I spoke up: 'I'm the one who gave you her photo, François.'

Laura turned towards me. 'Let me introduce the head cameraman for the video,' François said. 'He's also agreed to shoot the screen tests.'

Her eyes downcast, she stretched out her hand.

'I found your photo in a box lying around a production studio hallway. Have you been auditioning?'

'I don't remember.'

She was still holding the record jacket with Marc's photo on it. She held it up. 'Do you know him well?'

2

'I've known him for fifteen years,' I said. 'We went to school together.'

The office door opened. Marc entered first, saw Laura and waved, then stepped aside to let Omar pass. Omar walked over and stuck out his hand. I said, 'Laura, this is Omar Belamri. He's directing the video.'

Omar smiled at her, and said to me, 'I remember, you showed me her picture.'

Laura put the record jacket down, chewed on her nail, and said, 'But we've never met.'

I picked up the camera. Laura and Marc were side by side, leaning against a wall. I moved over, facing her, with Marc partly in frame to the left. Omar quickly explained the scene and told them to improvise: Laura would play a young prostitute in the port of Barcelona; Marc was her pimp. She looked into the lens; was she looking at me?

Marc spoke first: 'Who is this guy?'

'What guy?'

'I saw you.'

'I don't know him.'

'You don't know him? You're giving money to someone you don't know?'

'I didn't give him any money.'

'Are you putting me on, or what?'

She looked like a petulant little girl, but I could feel her fear. She bit her lips. 'Of course not.'

Using the electric zoom, I slowly moved in on her. Marc continued: 'I saw you slipping money to that little asshole.'

'What?'

'You give money to just anyone?'

'Me, give money? I never gave anybody money.'

Marc walked in front of her, ready to hit her. She took a

step back, a wary child. 'What do you want me to say?'

'I want you to tell me why you do this. Aren't you happy with me?'

'That's not it . . .'

'So who is he? A friend?'

'I don't know him.'

'You give him money, but you don't know him?'

'I do whatever I like with my money.'

'It isn't your money.'

Omar told me to cut. Marc and Laura took a break.

They sat down across from each other at a low table. I had removed the blue gels from the spots and switched the camera to 'artificial light'. Their faces took on a warm, orange color that made the cold outside even colder, the blue darker. Between the light of the fading day and that of the spotlights stretched the broad, smooth surface of the picture window.

'Pick up the same scene as before,' said Omar, 'but this time, Laura, you have the upper hand. You're going to dominate him.'

Marc spoke right away: 'I saw you with that guy, it's going to lead to trouble.'

'What do you want?'

She was looking at the lens and I again felt she was looking at me. 'What do you want me to tell you?'

Omar's voice: 'Tougher, be tougher.'

'I pulled you out of the gutter. You want to wind up back there?'

'I'll just find somebody else.'

'There won't be anyone else . . .'

'Zoom in on her,' Omar whispered in my ear. But Laura had stopped, blocked. She raised her head, looked at the

4

sky, said, 'It's the hour of the wolf,' then fell silent.

How did she know that expression? That way of describing the time between day and night, the moment we call 'magic time' in cinema.

As the outside light faded, I thought of those animal names that announce the coming of darkness: the hour of the wolf. I was searching in vain for another kind of animal name for later, for other hours and gestures, for full darkness.

I had left the office. I was alone, looking at the city through the viewfinder of the camera I had used to film Laura. In Stalingrad, a motionless old Arab, his hand on his fly, watched me walk by and get into my car. La Chapelle, the métro station with its tangle of stairs. Long tracking shots along the boulevards of Belleville and Ménilmontant lost to the night.

Night, an absence of light, but above all the denser mass of other lights, other colors. A pack of Marlboros bought at the African center on the rue Bisson. The big burlap bag the seller pulled the pack out of. A sideways glance, off to the left, towards a man in an overcoat who was about to cross in front of my car, half running, half skipping, a folded child's stroller on his shoulder bouncing up and down in time with his steps.

Superimposed over those images, mixed by an invisible control room, was Laura's child-woman face. How many of her fantasies had she had acted out? I wondered. How many men had already made her come?

In the rue de Belleville, I stepped into the Lao-Siam. The waiters and the owner shook my hand. I ordered Pho soup, a skewer of Thai shrimps, and a Tsing Tao. Sitting at the next table were two women of about thirty-five or forty and a younger guy who looked a bit shrunken, his short torso leaning above the paper tablecloth that was stained with soy sauce. The women were laughing constantly; the guy listened, his face young yet lined. One of the women was saying that a girlfriend had had her car towed away at two in the morning. She went to get it later, about seven. She pulled the car up to the exit of the pound. The license plate had come loose. The girl tried to open the door to get out, but the handle came off in her hand, and the door fell at the feet of the cop stationed at the gate. The cop's face had to be seen to be believed. Looking surprised, she walked over in her miniskirt, and very politely asked, 'Could you please tell me where I can get this repaired?'

'Young lady, you go into the first garage you come to and get this damned heap fixed.'

A loud thump from the rear of the car interrupted him. The girl rushed back, tried to kick the fallen muffler out of the cop's sight. Exasperated, he opened the gate and yelled, 'Climb back into that garbage can of yours and get the hell out of here!'

The two women were talking about the opening of the Palace. 'You'd just raise your little finger, and the guys would come running, remember?' The man at their table remained shrunken and silent.

I pictured Laura at thirteen, going out with men of thirty, dancing until six in the morning, smoking American cigarettes on the red steps of the Palace staircase, her eyes ringed by smoke and disgust.

I awoke with a start. Death was there, in the frightening shape of a pile of clothes on a chair at the foot of the bed, etched against the darkness by a ray of moonlight. Death had been there for two years now, every day, every minute, cutting me off from the world. My brain had turned to mush, darkened and compressed into a soft, shapeless mass like bloody ox lungs, crammed under my skull.

It had been there ever since the first articles about AIDS. I was immediately sure the disease would be a worldwide catastrophe which would carry me off along with other millions of the damned. From one day to the next, I changed my sexual practices. Before that, I had carefully sought out boys who pleased me and had them fuck me. From then on, I decided I wanted no more penetration, no more nights of love in a bed. I started going around the city looking for people like myself, who didn't want to come inside someone's body, whose spurting sperm fell onto dust in basements.

But masturbations alone soon no longer satisfied me. The obsessions of my adolescence returned: tight trouser crotches molding the shape of penises, piss-soaked under-wear . . . At school, when I was thirteen, I used to go into empty locker rooms, looking for shorts that had been forgotten or dropped by boys younger or slimmer than me. I'd take them home and put them on in front of the bathroom mirror. I don't think I was jerking off yet then; the pleasure of seeing the shape of my cock under the fabric came before orgasm. When I dared, I'd wear one of the stolen pairs of shorts to gym class, then feverishly wait for the boy's look to fall on the place between my legs . . .

To those adolescent obsessions, I now added leather, bonds, and pain. By bringing me suffering and release, they calmed the tension and terror created by the sickness.

I regularly headed for a shrine hungry for martyrs, a long arcade supported by square cement pillars on the left bank of the Seine between the Bercy and Austerlitz bridges. As in Plato's cave, light was perceived only by reflection, and the beings by their shadows. I went looking for depraved men, stiff cocks, degrading gestures, strong smells. Some bodies hesitated, circled, spoke; for me, it had to be all or nothing. I announced my tastes: if the answer was no, I roughly shoved the man away; if yes, I'd follow him and scream out my pleasure on the steps of an iron staircase on the other side of the bridge.

Standing soiled and bruised at the river's edge after orgasm, I felt graceful and light. Transparent.

*   *   *

Laura didn't get cast as Maria Teresa, the child-woman prostitute of Barcelona. Marc and Omar had considered her, but ended up choosing a well-known actress whose name would attract sponsors for the video.

I was somewhat relieved at not having to light Laura's face. I had imagined that it would absorb the light, a dark mass in which only her eyes would reflect anything.

The shoot was difficult. The producer had quarreled with Omar and didn't come to Barcelona. In his place, he sent an assistant producer, a completely inexperienced, very young woman who burst into tears at the slightest difficulty. On the harbor wharves, in the narrow streets and the gypsy bars of Chinatown, she cried a lot.

I liked working with Omar. I had first met him in a café in Les Halles; he was carrying an old brown leather briefcase. I've never doubted his talent, ever. For him, and for a few others, I would have been able to give a lot, without holding back, without having my stride broken by the sudden discovery of some imperfection in the other's body, face, or spirit.

I was aware of sinking deeper each day into a grave I was digging for myself, a glass- or mud-walled tomb that hid me from the world. I was less and less capable of communication, or of any relationship other than work or sex. Only talent could still unlock my generosity.

What little I know of Omar's past also drew me to him. A family of eleven children and the inevitable wrong turns; a couple of his brothers were delinquents, one was an epileptic. After fifteen years in the Nanterre slums, he alone escaped the booze and the Saturday-night bar fights. A hard, magnificent flower that managed to blossom in the garbage cans of the city.

I knew I'd never feel the desire to touch Omar's body. But if I had met one of his delinquent brothers, I would have moved heaven and earth to make out the shape of his cock under his jeans, spread his body, lay it across my sheets, have it close over me with anticipated tenderness, a surreal reversal of the hard, magnificent flower's blossoming.

*   *   *

When he'd finished editing *Maria Teresa*, Omar telephoned and asked me to meet him at the Etoile Verte. He'd been thinking about an idea for a screenplay, and suggested we write it together.

The story is set in the seventies, in the Nanterre slums, and revolves around Farid and his family. The war in Algeria has been over for eight years, but police raids are regular occurrences. The cops are always searching, smashing, shoving. Anything can happen here; the tension rarely lets up. Of course, life in the slum isn't just an endless succession of misfortune and sorrow, as some compassionate observer reflecting on the lives of those inside might imagine. There is also lightness, humor, moments of joy. When the rains come, and water leaks through the rusty tin roofs, and rivers of mud flow between the shacks, the memory of the sun lives on in some unknown chromosome carried by the slum kids, glowing within them with a special radiance.

Those homosexuals who dare come to cruise along the edge of the slum. For the young Algerians, it's a game; for the men who desire muscular bodies and dark eyes, it's a tragedy endlessly repeated.

Farid and his mate Hassan are both fourteen. They secretly befriend Jean, who is twenty-five. Jean first met Farid one evening when he was wandering not far from the slum; he came on to him, felt him up a little. Farid came very quickly in his pants. Jean slipped him a bill. Ashamed, Farid ran away. Jean returns; he sees Farid again, this time with Hassan, but doesn't try to touch them. They talk. Jean tells them he works with the Paris public transit agency; Farid and Hassan try to get free passes from him.

One day when they're going to meet Jean, Farid and

Hassan spot him from afar, surrounded by a group of twenty-year-olds which includes Khaled, one of Farid's brothers. Fists fly, they knock Jean to the ground, steal everything he has, and leave him unconscious, bleeding, his clothes ripped. When the big boys leave, Farid and Hassan approach, gingerly touch him with their fingertips. Jean comes to. His face is covered with blood and he isn't able to stand: his right ankle is sprained, and his foot dangles limply. The kids are frightened, but Jean says it's nothing, it will be all right. He knows, because he's a doctor. He lied to them when he said he worked with the transit agency. He laughs; that's why they're still waiting for their free passes!

Jean asks Farid to take him to his parents' place so he can clean himself up. The boys look at each other. A fag in their place? 'They'd kill us!' So they drag Jean along a road, drop him near a level crossing, set off the alarm and run for cover. From their hiding place, they see a car stop; the driver picks Jean up and lays him across the rear seat.

Later, Farid tries to talk with his brother Khaled, tells him he saw him and his friends beating up a guy. Khaled just laughs: 'You aren't starting to stand up for fags, are you?'

Farid says he understands why they robbed him, but there wasn't any reason to destroy the guy. Khaled gets angry: 'Do you know that guy? What have you been doing with him?'

Farid denies knowing Jean. Khaled believes him. Before leaving to meet Marly, his waiting girlfriend, he says, 'The French have done a lot worse.'

A few days later, Farid's family is together at the dinner table. The door to the shack door opens, and there's Jean, standing in the doorway, his face covered with bruises. He says hello, puts a package of medicine on the table, says it's

11

for the family. Then he walks over to Farid, kisses him on the forehead, and tells him he isn't coming back. He's flying to Damascus to offer his services to the Palestinian revolution, caring for wounded fedayeen. He tells the family not to blame Farid; they didn't do anything bad together.

The film closes with some text, in white letters on a black background, just before 'The End': 'Doctor Jean Valade was taken prisoner on King Hussein's orders and tortured to death in a Jordanian prison.'

I had never written a screenplay before, but Omar knew about my life, my loves, and my friendships. He had lived in the slums, had been Farid. He suspected that I could get inside Jean's head, Jean who was completely at the mercy of his desire for Arab bodies, unable to withhold anything from them. He could even enlist in one of their revolutions. But every one of Jean's gestures and actions reeked of Judeo-Christianity; he would die at the hands of Arabs, Arab hands killing other Arabs. As for me, I never had the courage to give myself to any revolution whatsoever.

*   *   *

Carol and Kader were the last vestiges of my former love life. I had known Carol for eight years; we had first met at a ski resort. Thinking it was the way to keep me, she had accepted everything: my attraction to boys; the transparent, beautiful young men who were my first lovers; the arrogant toughs who followed; my sexual fantasies, which I thought she shared, but in fact were an unbearable chore for her. She played a risky game, and lost. We hardly ever saw each other anymore, and the idea of caressing her or making love to her disgusted me.

Kader was a handsome, eighteen-year-old Algerian I had known for more than two years. I met him outside a movie theater on place Clichy; I had pushed open the door, and he was outside on the pavement, wearing a flowered shirt and smiling in the June sunshine. He had asked me for the time.

I shared some beautiful memories with Kader; nights of love-making when he took me and I cried out with pleasure; the rocks near the Antibes harbor where we slept under the stars; the sight of his body as he battled the ocean waves while I waited for him on the sands of the Chambre d'Amour.

But I had been too busy anticipating the moment when I would distance myself to realize how attached to him I had become. In the beginning, sex exalted our love; later, the two merged. Then came the threat of illness. I didn't tell Kader about the terrors that obsessed me, just gave myself to him less and less often, without explanation. I was afraid of infecting him, and afraid he might infect me, if he hadn't already.

Our love was already slowly disintegrating when it was put to the test by a trip: I followed Kader to Algeria. I came back loveless; or rather with a love that had been razed, as thoroughly destroyed as the houses of El Esnam, where we had lived, had been demolished by an earthquake.

The AIDS test was just becoming generally available in Paris then, and I was advised to see a specialist at the Necker Hospital. He felt the nodes at the base of my throat and along my jugular. I was looking out the window; the day was as gray as a bad smile. Turning my head toward the doctor, I saw in his eyes that he knew. 'We'll order the test.'

I got the results two weeks later: I was HIV-positive. A white, freezing wave washed along my arms and legs. In the room, the doctor's reassuring words faded to a distant murmur.

A few hours later, I felt almost relieved. Not knowing had been the worst. Everything had changed, yet everything was exactly the same as before.

Though I wondered who had infected me, I blamed only myself. I saw blurred faces, quickly replaced by the image of the virus: a jagged ball covered with spikes, like a medieval mace.

Omar found financing for the film we had written together, and asked me to light and shoot it. I accepted with pleasure and the preparations began. Kader tried out for the role of Khaled, but Omar - correctly - didn't pick him. Khaled, whom Omar and I had invented, was an outlaw; his implacable violence put him beyond our rules. Kader, on the other hand, wanted to belong, so he could take his revenge in broad daylight.

I saw my enforced absence from Kader as a chance to break with him completely.

*   *   *

I was having dinner with Omar, who had a faraway look in his eyes, and was rolling a burned-out cigarette with a chewed filter along his lips. He said he couldn't find anybody to play Marly, Khaled's French girlfriend. I didn't even need to think: the sentence just burst from my lips: 'Ring Laura!' Omar didn't hear me correctly, made me repeat. 'For the role of Marly, ask Laura.'

'The one who tried out for *Maria Teresa*?'

'Yes.'

For me, something about the restaurant's horizon suddenly jerked out of kilter. I again saw Laura's eyes, in extreme close-up, through my camera's viewfinder: a pale face in black and white, glowing from within as from a dark flame. I thought of a tawny color, a savage color linked to another word that hadn't been revealed. Laura hadn't revealed herself either, covered as she was with a black veil only I could see. Among some peoples, blue is the color of mourning; so black doesn't indicate only death. It means the absence of image. With Laura's face masked, one of my possible lives was also hidden.

Omar telephoned Laura, who asked him to send her a script.

She didn't get back to him, so he rang her again, and I listened in on an extension. She seemed ill at ease, said she wasn't sure she could play Marly. Omar pressed her. Finally, she admitted that her mother didn't want her to take the part. 'Arabs and fags, it's a bit much for her!'

So Laura was a minor, then. She had lied when François had asked her age; without hesitation, she had answered 'Eighteen.' I had guessed she might be given to lying. I suspected she didn't lie for a specific purpose. Her lying

15

was more vague, more global; it was a variation on the truth, a way of dressing up reality to enliven it. It was also a way of shattering equilibrium, of putting everyone, including herself, off balance.

*   *   *

On the evening of the last day of shooting, we went to a Levallois pizzeria for the traditional dinner to celebrate the end of filming. The tech crew and the actors were seated at tables arranged in a semicircle. Eric, the actor who had played Jean – the homosexual doctor who went to join Arafat's forces – was sitting across from me. Our glances met often and lingered.

I decided to approach him. With my mouth close to his ear, I said, 'I want you.'

'I was thinking the same thing.'

I went out the back door of the pizzeria. There were stairs, arcades, housing projects all around. Eric came out to join me; kisses and hugs. Holding each other tightly, we rolled around in the stairway landings of modern apartment buildings, against cars, lit by the orange glow of the sodium-vapor streetlights. A love glimpsed, stolen moments.

And then, once again, it all turned into an absurd series of self-defeating gestures and words.

A first night of lovemaking. A cup of coffee near the plaza at Les Halles with Bertrand and Djemila, a woman friend of Eric's. Bertrand bought some postcards and gave me one of a boy pissing against a wall, wearing a white shirt and floppy pants, a cap on his head, his face turned towards the camera.

Thinking about that name, Djemila, I could see the orange of a setting sun, with darkness gradually falling across Kabylie in north-east Algeria. But rip away that first veil, and a very different vision appears, one awash in bloody red and the mutilated bodies history has piled near the town of Djemila, brought together in my memory in the Cuicul ruins.

In the fourth century, the first bodies fell under the blows of the ragtag 'fighters for Christ' hired by the Donatists to slake their thirst for martyrs. Sixteen hundred years later, on 9 May 1945, more bodies were hacked to bits at the same place: the bodies of French colonials besieged by the Algerians, drunk with humiliations, who took the celebration of victory over Germany as a chance to turn history around. Crushed skulls, children with slashed faces, raped women with bellies slit open, men with their genitals stuffed into their mouths.

In the fourth century, the Catholics had cried, 'Deo gratias!' The dissident Donatists, the Puritans, the rampaging Moors and the anarchist peasants yelled, 'Deo laudes!' But in 1945, a new cry galvanized the young rebels: 'El Jihad!' The holy war.

Other bodies joined them, Arab bodies, ten times as numerous, murdered during the blind repression of May 1945. It was a precursor of the first ambushes of 1954 and the war that followed.

'We don't want bread, we want blood.' I was obsessed by the slogan, repeated a thousand times, yelled by the rioters to the emissaries from the regional capital, the mixed community of Fedj-M'zala, eight hundred yards

17

from the village, near the bridge over the Bouslah wadi.

I wanted blood instead of bread, too. But I wanted fresh blood, clear and free-flowing, miraculously washed clean of the poison that was spreading in it.

*   *   *

Eric phoned often, dropped in to see me on the film sets where I was working. One day, coming back from a trip to Lille, I found him sitting on a café terrace opposite from the Gare du Nord, near where I had chained my motorcycle to a pole. We threw ourselves into each other's arms. I so believed in our love, I even accepted its conventional rounds: the Trouville quay, the Honfleur harbor, the bar at the Grand Hotel in Cabourg, the Houlgate casino terrace in the morning, under the September sun.

But as winter closed in on Paris, a metallic sky defeated us; metal without the brilliant chrome of September, just heavy and gray, a tin sky, a zinc sky, ready to rust in the first rain.

I was at the Lao-Siam, my solitary retreat, thinking of Eric, who had flown to London. A man and a woman were having dinner at the next table, sitting opposite each other. He looked appealing, despite a mustache and oily hair, and she was quite pretty. He was telling her about his wife, who had left him three years before. So this is the timelessness of love: repeated absences or conversations in bars or Chinese restaurants. The man's ex-wife had paid him a visit during his vacation on the Basque coast. She was in love with another man. Of her former lover, she had said, 'Oh, I dropped him in a minute!' The man had screamed, 'Christ! I nearly blew my brains out fifty times in three years because of that guy, and you have the nerve to tell me you dropped him in a minute!'

I frightened myself. Was this all I was good for, working and stealing snatches of talk from neighboring tables at night? I wanted laughter and lightness, not the depression I had sunk into, nor the lethargy which overcame me at the prospect of having to force myself to talk to someone.

Had Eric made love to Djemila? I wondered. Djemila – Djamel for a man – were names which even at rest suggested warfare and hidden violence.

Eric's own war was of another kind. He wanted to revenge himself, of course: on poverty, on the parents who abandoned him, on the deserted Haute-Loire where the only face he saw was that of the old peasant woman who had brought him up.

But above all, Eric needed to seduce. He was a perfect mirror of the age; twenty years earlier, he wouldn't have been the same person, and certainly not an actor. He confused the satisfaction of his narcissism with artistic creativity.

I didn't tell Eric about the virus coursing in my veins. But I was in no danger of infecting him, either. We jerked each other off; he didn't fuck me, and I didn't fuck him.

Each of us caressed the traces of his lost adolescence on the other's body.

*   *   *

True to form, Eric gradually drifted away over endless discussions at cafés, trying to convince me that there was more than one way to love someone. Then he would get up and leave, a slightly stiff figure walking on the pavement, his strides a little too short.

On the morning of the last night we spent together, he asked me to take him back to his place, that is, to the apartment he shared with a guy I had several times heard crying on the phone. I refused; I couldn't bear the idea of giving Eric over to someone's body other than mine.

He pulled on a jacket, paced the floor. 'If it were me, and I had a car, I'd take you home, and that would be that.' He picked up the phone and called for a taxi. Without looking at me, he yelled, 'You don't know me, pal!' I tried to stop him; he stormed out, slamming the door.

*   *   *

I was ready for anything, which is to say, nothing. I didn't have a penny and was taking any job that came my way. I ended up in Mulhouse for a week, shooting news stories for the local FR3 station.

The first night, lying on the bed in my hotel room, I

noticed a Bible on the side table. I opened it and absently thumbed through the pages. On the endpaper I found a passionate declaration of love written by one Armand to a certain Juliet, who, of course, would never read it. Others, like me, read it instead, the random recipients of an excess of love.

I thought of Eric. 'You aren't waiting for me,' I said aloud. 'You won't be there when I get back. But what you don't know, and what I want you to know, is that each time you refuse me your love, I will sink a little lower, to convince myself that other loves don't exist, that other embraces all turn sour.'

I was in pain, but in a city drenched with orange rain and cut by broken lines of metal, the suffering reminded me that I was alive. Seeking filth, smearing and soiling my body with it, summoned a pain that I preferred to inaction. My bruised body lay spread-eagled on the cement of the quay. It was me, battered in body and soul.

*   *   *

I saw Eric again. We went to the movies on the Champs-Elysées. On the film's soundtrack, I heard phrases we had once said to each other.

It was night when we came out, and a blackout had plunged the avenue into darkness. Eric drew close, brushed against me; glances exchanged, time stopped. I believed our love had returned, or the illusion of it.

But the lights on the avenue came on again and broke the spell. Eric climbed on the motorcycle behind me, and I brought him back to Montmartre. During the trip, he laid his hands on my thighs and on my gloved hands.

I wanted to kiss him when we parted, wanted him to kiss me, to prolong the moment, but got only a furtive peck. 'I'll call you,' he said. I tried to delay him; 'What can I do?'

'I've felt better since telling you it's over, and that isn't going to change.' He moved away, walking across place Blanche.

Sunday afternoon. Eric rang the doorbell, and I let him in. He got undressed, undressed me, stretched out on my bed.

We made love. I lay against his skin but at the same time hovered in the air above our intertwined bodies. Disbelieving, I watched a scene in which I was one of the partners.

*　　*　　*

I screwed a camera into my hollow eye socket, where the memory of Eric flickered. It moved through the night, registering only the brightest lights.

In contrast to the grayness of the under-exposed video image, cocaine seemed the purest white. A sharp jab that pierced the nasal passages and lodged directly in the brain. I started doing a lot of coke in those days.

I would walk through the city, always preceded by my video camera, my back and shoulder muscles in spasm, my heart racing at 116 beats a minute.

Back at my place, I would take more cocaine. At six o'clock in the morning, I closed the shutters and drew the curtains so as not to see the light of dawn. Already, I could hardly stand its pale, dirty light. It made me feel guilty.

To get to sleep, I had to come first: shoot my load into my pants, on the fly of my jeans, or onto my hairless belly. It was the same dirty white that was assaulting my windows. Day was coming on to the glass, the sperm of dawn was dripping down the façade to the foot of the building.

Was it after one of those nights that I created that last scene with Eric? Or had I filmed it, concentrating my new suffering into the centre of the image?

No. We actually lived it. I see a low wall above the Seine and the expressway along the right bank between the Garigliano and Bir Hakeim bridges. We were sitting on the wall, Eric and I, side by side, our faces turned towards each other, close enough to touch, illuminated by the spotlights from the river-boats; but infinitely far apart as well, separated by a cold fog and the loud roar of the cars driving by below.

I was stroking his face. He drew back, and my fingers were left hanging in the air, arrows without a target.

'Stop,' he muttered.

'Do I disgust you?'

'Don't start that again.'

'Are you meeting someone? Is he waiting for you?'

'I'm living with someone,' he said. 'I live with him. It's a decision I've made, can you understand that?'

'What about me?'

'You do as I do, you wait. You wait for the right moment.'

'Last Sunday, you were the one who crawled into my

bed in the middle of the afternoon. I didn't ask you for anything.'

'I wanted to see. I don't understand why there isn't anything left. I don't know why . . . This is ridiculous, I told myself. So I tried.'

'And so? Is there anything left?'

'I don't know.'

After a long silence, I said, 'I'm losing more than you are.'

'I'm losing a love story, too,' he answered.

The next day, the ring of the phone woke me. It was Laura, calling to tell me that she knew of a director who was looking for a cameraman for a short film, and that she had given him my name and number.

Lying next to Eric's body, I had forgotten about Laura's face. And here she was, calling me the day after I broke up with him; I couldn't help but take it as a sign.

When I met the director, I couldn't understand why he wanted to be a film-maker. Our needs were different. Or rather, he didn't have any needs; my only need was to find a reason for going on. Reality was my drug; in order to transform it, to turn it into something I could shoot into my veins, poetry was essential. A phrase kept running through my mind: 'The Panthers won because of poetry.'

I wanted to give myself to some great cause, without knowing which one to choose, or how to go about choosing it. Something stopped me, hobbled me. I was chained, a slave to shameful nights. When would I start living the life of a mercenary or a bomber?

The pay wasn't much and the script didn't interest me, but the shoot was to take place in Morocco, and I wanted to leave, to head for the sun, to forget Eric. Driven by some obscure force, of which Laura was somehow a part, I accepted the director's offer.

*   *   *

A few days before my departure for Morocco, I got an invitation to a party thrown by a film production company. I had been going out less and less lately, but decided to accept. The party was being given at the company's headquarters near the place de la République. The crowd was pretty much what I expected: an array of more or less parasitic insects: chic 'creative types', dirty and unshaven; stylish crustaceans convinced of the richness of their inner universe and of the futility of trying to share it; and a few former militant Trotskyites who had moved into advertising or journalism.

I slowly made my way through the crowd to a large metal table set up as a bar. There seemed to be nothing to drink but tequila. I poured myself a glass and heard a few words exchanged by two women standing next to me.

'I'm just dying to have him!'

'Forget it. Hervé's gay!'

'Bullshit! Stan spreads that kind of garbage around because he tried to fuck him last year in London and Hervé wouldn't go along.'

'He's been keeping a Paki dish dog for the past two years.'

'You mean someone who works in a kennel?'

'No, silly, a kid who washes dishes in a restaurant!'

'So how do you explain Ariane's spending a night in his bed at the Normandy? I haven't heard her complaining!'

I walked off without waiting to hear the rest, moving towards the center of the room where the dancers were jumping around, zigzagging between the crush of bodies. And suddenly I saw him, in the space left by the departure of a big guy in a white jacket. He was completely trashed, dancing a sort of anemic pogo. Serge was bearing down on me with the eyes and manners of a piranha and the body of a wild boar, but I pretended not to notice. 'Ciao, bello!' he shouted. 'Is that Sammy you're staring at like that? A word to the wise: forget it. I know it all by heart. He was a nice piece three years ago, but he's nineteen now, much too old . . . He's still got a nice ass, but since he wears baggy pants, you can't see a thing.'

I grunted something to Serge, who was trying to feel me up. As usual, you couldn't tell what was true from what he was making up, any more than you could tell when he believed the role he was playing and when he was making fun of himself.

'I made a film for Renault, and they gave me a car. You'll never guess what number plate it's got: "FLN 75!"* You can imagine how that impresses the Arabs when I go cruising out on the edge of town. By the way, I've never taken you on a grand tour of the underground, have I? You

---

* FLN – Front de Libération National, the Algerian independence movement. (*Translator's note*)

didn't know that in the basements of housing projects around Paris people are screwing their brains out, did you? You have to know the times and places, and it's mainly boys fucking girls, but sometimes they go with guys.'

Serge was still talking, but I kept looking at Sammy. 'You really seem to like him,' Serge said. 'I'll introduce you.'

The evening continued, exactly the same, but meeting Sammy had suddenly illuminated it. His eyes were a mix of seduction, irony, and curiosity; his hard, fleshy mouth was beautiful. I imagined him awash in betrayal.

We drank and danced. As a liquor, tequila is both transparent and metallic, so it was metal, filtered by our blood and mixed with our sweat, that soaked our T-shirts. Maybe that's why the metal particles suspended in the spotlights suddenly began to glitter; I had the impression that a word was rising up within me, freed from the tongue's procession, moving alone under a gold and amber halo: the word 'savage'. Sammy was a savage. And the halo above the word suggested holiness.

I wasn't thinking of the great predators, standing on their tall legs; my savages are short, solid and muscular. They lean against walls, one leg bent, one foot flat against the cement, their slightly turned heads bowed, eyes looking up. Or, more rarely, they're girls, always in movement. They walk away, suddenly stop, turn their heads, and you catch their eye through the still-swinging curls of their hair.

The savages' violence is contained, tangled, twisted in on itself. It's hidden along their backbones, where you can lay your cheek, and feel their power.

Amid the alcoholic fumes and the throb of the dancing, by a poetic leap, I associated the word 'savage' with my nights of humiliation.

My descents into the underworld were nothing but shadow-plays; the asses, tits, cocks, and bellies I squeezed belonged to no one. Words, especially, were banished, except for the imperious demands for immediate gratification of some desire. All the others rang false to me, like parodies of the conversations on the surface.

We were shadows among the shadows, and needed more than our delicate sense of touch to locate the bodies in that infernal darkness. Our bodies' shadows had to be darker than night itself, but the desired body's mass of darkness had to cast a shadow in order to stand out against the lighter darkness around it. But for a shadow to be cast, there had to be a light source up there, at the surface. That light, as bright as the sun for me, was given to us by the savages. Sammy and others of his race were shining lights, and I worshipped them as Heliogabalus once had.*

Then, when the savage stars had set, or were exhausted or absent, the cyclical nights of perversion returned. Did Sammy and the other savages have their own sun, or did they draw warmth from the night they gave out, as it was reflected back at them? Were they marching towards some vanishing point, carrying me to some apex?

For me, the horizon was only illness. On that unrelieved flatness I saw an image of myself, microscopic in size. On the horizon, I was nothing but a virus.

* Heliogabalus: a third-century Roman emperor whose profligacy rivaled Caligula's. (*Tr.*)

I was drunk. I thought I saw the ghost of Gottfried Benn moving towards me. He grabbed my shoulder and murmured, 'Poetry isn't born of meaning, and it doesn't echo any values. There isn't anything before or after it. It is the object that is.'

I wanted Benn to let go, yelled that he was no poet, but the specter hung on. 'A double life,' he said, 'as I've proposed theoretically and lived in practice, is a conscious, systematic, tendentious split of the personality.'

Having left the party, we were defenseless. Sammy was vomiting into the gutter, I was bouncing off parked cars. Serge walked away, holding the arm of a young Kabyle he was taking to a country house a friend had lent him for the night.

Benn's ghost came out on to the street; 'Living signifies experiencing life and getting something artificial from it,' he shrieked in my ear.

All I had got from life was a death sentence. The ghost pulled me close, and I struggled, trying to escape his embrace. A face floated into my field of vision and leaned against the hollow of my shoulder: Sammy. He existed. He hugged me in his arms.

I was living in a studio on the seventeenth floor of an apartment complex. Sammy and I walked to the elevator, holding each other up. I opened my front door and immediately went to collapse on the bed.

As Sammy got undressed, I watched his magnificently muscular body. He felt me looking. 'You like boys?' he asked.

'There's only one bed, but you can share it. I won't rape you.'

'An Amsterdam train conductor fucked me when I was thirteen. I'm not a fag, but it doesn't really bother me.'

Lying there naked, we gradually slipped closer. Sammy was proud of his body. At first, he let me caress him. He got a hard-on before I did. Then we kissed, and his hands moved over my skin, my cock, my ass. My eyes were closing, but I moved my lips down over his nipples, his chest, his belly, his cock. He came in my mouth with a shout.

I had a headache when I awoke, but hauled myself out of bed to pack my bags. Sammy was still asleep; he was lying on his stomach, the sheets molding the hollow of his back and the curved mound of his ass.

What was this boy doing in my bed? I wondered. His body, his skin, his gestures and his mouth clearly belonged to someone who liked women. But I wouldn't be able to seduce him by accentuating my femininity.

Once revealed, my love for Sammy would be doomed, I knew. But that contradiction fascinated me. The thing that would kill this love had nothing to do with the usual reasons: a gesture, a word, a tone of voice, a detail of the body, a way of dressing, the silliness or greediness of boys whose homosexuality is too flagrant.

Wanting to love Sammy was a way of joining a global battle, becoming part of history. That battle, I thought, would lead to others, battles in the service of some great cause I wanted desperately to serve, but hadn't yet found.

Or did I believe that by some psychosomatic mechanism, the battle could generate beneficient genes that would mutuate the deadly aberration I carried in my blood?

When Sammy woke up, he asked me to drive him to his parents' house in the southern suburbs. I told him I had to catch a plane for Casablanca in two hours. I'd call for a taxi and drop him off at the Porte d'Italie. Apart from a few grunts, he kept quiet until he'd drunk the coffee I made for him.

In the taxi, he answered my questions evasively. By the time he got out, I knew only that he had returned to Paris two months before after doing his military service with the mountain troops. He had originally enlisted for five years, but resigned after six months. He was working part-time on a community job training program at the Bastille opera. He was Spanish on his mother's side, Arab on his father's. And he was living with a thirty-five-year-old woman, a journalist for a leftist weekly. Sammy walked away, and I headed to the airport for my plane to Morocco.

On takeoff, I was surprised to realize that I wasn't as frightened as usual; the threat of a terminal illness was putting my fears in perspective.

The previous night had given me strange visions, I thought. Sammy and the ghost of Gottfried Benn face to face. On the one hand, the simple body of a radiant half-caste boy full of suppressed violence. On the other, a cynical, tortured spirit, condemned as a formalist by both the Nazis and their enemies. Benn was closer to the former, but less because he believed in Hitlerian dogma than because when his kind of outlook becomes corrupted, it gives rise to Nazism.

*   *   *

I met the director at Mohammedia, and we started scouting locations. He didn't know what he wanted, but his doubts had nothing to do with creative uncertainty. He irritated me tremendously, and I had to go to great lengths to keep it from being too obvious. He wanted me to believe that film-making was the logical extension of the decadence of his disintegrating upper-middle-class family. He would fill the camera's empty field of vision with clichés.

We were staying at the Cynthia, a luxury hotel from the seventies which had seen better days. It was rarely full, except when besieged by tour groups. The two-story hotel was depressing, but in a way that was different from other decaying palaces; it had no history. Its rooms had doors that opened onto balconies overlooking a huge covered patio, as vacant as its memory. Mustard-colored walls and ugly orange carpets were marks of man's passage through an overwhelming ocean of sadness.

The emptiness of the hotel bordered on the metaphysical, and I suggested to the director that we shoot a series of scenes there. He was drunk on Boulaoune wine and hesitated, then finally said, 'It isn't in the script, and anyway, I didn't come to Morocco to shoot in some hotel I could have found in Paris or Hamburg.'

Sunk in a deckchair next to the pool, I had the feeling I was going through life the way American tourists go through countries on their itinerary: full-tilt, so as to 'do' as many cities as possible. I was completely alone.

I no longer attracted adventures. I had once had the knack of adapating myself to any situation. It had saved my life a few times; I had come back unscathed from places where I could have died. 'Come back,' the way you come back from hell or from beyond the grave for sex, the illusion of love, the brutal reality of different people's lives. In order to see, to discover, I had let myself slide so far down I forgot which way was up. In the depths, I made no judgments. Like a dog who can smell someone's fear and often bites him, my rough trade can spot someone who isn't with them body and soul, who still clings to his world by a gesture, a word, a look, his clothes, or a certain stiffness of his body.

'Body and soul.' An unfortunate phrase; body and soul are one. When Kader used to fuck me, even at El Esnam when our love died, he penetrated first my body, but beyond that, within himself, it was my soul that his cock pierced.

I used to be able to take my time, let myself go into life, and then, once the experience was over, to reflect on it. But I was already in perpetual motion, even then. Saggitarians are constantly on the move. I saw this as a kind of protective reflex, that made me flee people or places the moment they were touched by conformity or the established order. If anyone had power over me, it drove me mad; it seemed sweeter when I had power over someone else.

Driven by a kind of frenzy, my constant need for novelty had finally put everything out of my reach. This addiction to motion, which for me was an instinct for self-preservation, was freezing me in total immobility: where do you go when you think you've already been everywhere?

*   *   *

We finished the shoot, and I don't remember a thing about it. People probably moved around and in front of the camera, against African landscapes and a milky blue sky. The crew split up; the Moroccans went home and the French returned to Paris. I decided to stay on, to hire a car and drive around. Three days later, I telephoned the lab: developing the rushes had apparently gone smoothly, but a scratch had appeared on the negatives of two series of takes. Creating images is part of my job, and it terrified me to think that an invisible mote of dust, a tiny grain of sand lost in the inner workings of the camera, had obliterated whole scenes of love, death, war and betrayal. A painter can erase or rip up his canvas and start his representation of the world all over again, but a film-maker is chained to the crushing weight of his chosen tool, with its dozens of intermediaries and considerable sums of money.

I was driving, but I felt like an American actor playing a scene inside a car on a Hollywood set. I could see the road, the sky, and the landscape rolling by, but they had no more reality than stock images being projected behind the rear window of a 1950 Plymouth.

Then I reached the Atlas range and everything changed. The daylight was fading. Dark clouds were building above the Tizi n' Tichka mountains as I climbed to meet them.

I gave a lift to a hitchhiking amethyst seller. I was driving fast, and he gripped the edges of his seat in fear.

34

Between his frightened silence and the shouts of a radio sports reporter doing a play-by-play commentary on a Mundial soccer match stretched all the space in the world. Climbing the steps leading to the roof of this world, just below the leaden clouds, I was sure that new portents awaited me on the other side of the mountain.

At Tamlalte, when it's very hot, you can see honey flowing in the cracks in the rocks. Pink flowers bloom there winter and summer. In June, the women work the fields; afterwards, the men take their places.

The locals, tired of waiting for the state to make good its promise to bring electricity to the area – a promise it makes every year, and never keeps – had chipped in to buy an electric generator. By its feeble light, I walked down the narrow alleys of the douar one night, guided by the piercing sound of music. It was the last day of Ramadan, and a celebration was underway in the village square.

The young people were dancing; the girls wore their best clothes, jewelry and make-up; the boys pounded on wide, flat drums or on oil cans that had been cut in half; little children ran this way and that. The dancers were arrayed in two parallel lines, the girls facing the boys. Taking tiny steps, they advanced and retreated together, then spun around. Children who couldn't keep time were shooed aside.

One of the boys would sing something out, and all the others picked it up. Then the girls repeated the line in turn. In the responses, the singers would change a word or two of the original phrase. The lines were made up of simple words; the boy who initiated one would put his life into it, his little daily frustrations, his reverses in love. If two boys coveted the same 'gazelle', they would challenge each other, each singing his own praises and pointing out his rival's faults.

At first, I thought the phrases were composed on the spot. Later, I learned they had been prepared beforehand. Not that they had been completely written in advance, but they couldn't be spoken by just anyone: the boys who sang them had been chosen. By this choice, the other inhabitants of the douar had accorded them the title of poet.

Then, just like in any other city of the world where your upstairs neighbor starts banging on the door because the music at your party is too loud, the dance was stopped by a crazy old guy who was bothered by the noise. He climbed on to a roof, unscrewed the lone electric bulb shining its pale light on the dance, and smashed it on the ground. There were a few shouts, but no one got angry at the old geezer. Having become shadows of themselves, the dancers dispersed. I went to bed.

Back in Casablanca, I stopped at a hotel, the Laughing Boar. It seemed empty, almost deserted. A beautiful Frenchwoman in her fifties with long gray hair was sitting in the empty dining room, knitting. I asked for a room; she looked up, told me that all the rooms were free, and named a ridiculously low price. A Moroccan boy came in, walked over behind the woman, and put his hands on her shoulders. She turned her face towards him and they smiled at each other. He was more than handsome; his radiance filled the empty room. The look they exchanged was magnificent, too. What sacred happiness, born of

36

defying God-knows-what taboos, had I disturbed by coming here?

Lying down in my room, a series of blurred images unfolded before my eyes: a knitting-needles ballet, an insect's legs as it climbed a dune, skittering on the sliding grains of sand, the hands of the Tamlalte musicians pounding their drums. I fell asleep and woke at eight in the evening.

I ate dinner alone under the staring eyes of a stuffed boar's head. Mounting part of a wild pig as a hunting trophy struck me as an ultimate colonial affront to the Moslem world. It was a wasted effort. France had been blown away from here by a tornado, probably that of the love between the gray-haired woman and the Moroccan boy.

She had taken my order and given it to an Arab woman of about her age who was standing by the doors to the kitchen. Then the Frenchwoman, whose name was Madame Thévenet, went and sat down in front of the young Moroccan and continued her dinner. The Arab woman went into the kitchen.

There was nothing French about the food that was served, either. I was eating watermelon for dessert when the door opened and a man of about thirty came in, carrying a suitcase and an overnight bag.

Everything about him shouted, 'European'. He was serious, responsible, parading his origins and his power – and profoundly boring. He made his way to the table where the gray-haired woman and the young Moroccan were eating, and said loudly, 'How are you, mother?'

She got up, turned her face for him to kiss, and answered very softly, 'I'm fine. How are you? Did you have a good trip?'

37

He answered her, still in the same loud voice. Not a word or a glance for the young Moroccan, who, though he was seated, overwhelmed him with his beauty and his radiant body.

'Sit down, Kheira will get you something.'

'Thanks, mother, I've eaten.'

He waved at me from afar. Driven by some stupid impulse – considering that I had immediately found him repellant – I spoke instead of nodding. 'Good evening,' I said. 'Did you come from Paris?'

My sentence seemed ridiculous, spoken as if I had been holed up at the Laughing Boar for weeks, trapped near a jungle at the ends of the earth by a raging revolution, and that he had had to dodge bullets and cross fields of corpses to reach us.

'From Paris? Good lord, no! I could never stand living there. I live in the country near Biarritz.'

He walked toward me as he spoke, and introduced himself: 'Patrick Thévenet.'

I gestured for him to sit down at my table. 'Would you like something to drink?' I asked.

He asked for a whiskey. Kheira, the Arab woman, set a dusty bottle on the table.

'This is your first visit, isn't it?'

'To Morocco?'

'No, to the Laughing Boar.'

'Yes, it is.'

'You should have seen it in its glory days. The hotel used to belong to my father, Roland Thévenet. All Casablanca used to come through here. People stood in line to eat at his place. And the bashes he used to throw! My father cut quite a broad swath, you know.'

'Did he ever go back to France?'

'No, he died here. He got food poisoning from some canned Spanish food he ate on the way from France.'

'I'm sorry . . .'

'We were all here when he died. It hit him right after he arrived; we were eating couscous. We called a French doctor, but it was no use. My father was in terrible pain when he died. He said that his guts were burning up inside him, that his belly was devouring him.'

During the silence that followed, I caught Kheira giving Patrick Thévenet a veiled look full of hate. He went on talking, but much more quietly. 'My mother stayed on . . . I suppose you've probably guessed why.'

He had said, 'why', but I was sure he was thinking, 'for whom'. He obviously considered the young Moroccan unfit for membership of the human race; he was just a stiff cock that penetrated his mother every night.

I chose to play along. 'What is his name?'

'Mustapha, I think. You could write a novel about people like my father.'

Later, after several drinks, Thévenet rattled on about the things I expected of him: his brilliant career in public works; his hatred of Algeria, which had 'fallen to the Russians'; the Palais-Royal gardens defaced by Buren's columns; France's decadence. He told of a woman friend who had been shopping for dressers in the souks of Marrakesh. To cut short a bargaining session with a merchant, she had told him they were too expensive. The man had answered, 'Are you one of François Mitterand's new poor?' 'Before, no Moroccan would ever have dared say something like that,' Thévenet concluded. 'France's image abroad has slipped pretty badly, hasn't it?'

I got up, said good-night to Thévenet and his mother.

'Kheira is making a couscous for noon tomorrow,' she said. 'If you're still here, please have lunch with us.' I thanked her, saying I didn't know where I would be at noon tomorrow. With Kheira's eyes on me, I glanced at Mustapha and went out.

I got undressed and took a shower. As I was drying myself off, I spotted a purple blotch on my left biceps. 'It can't be,' I muttered. 'It can't be that . . .'

In bed, I couldn't sleep. I could feel death approaching, two images mixed together: an abstract, smooth one of death, and one etched with Laura's eyes. And this death wasn't mine, even if its smell reminded me it was waiting for me with open arms, its secrets bared. A blood-red flower under my skin.

With the feeling that something extraordinary was going to happen, Laura returned to my memory; as if she were pulling invisible threads, writing my destiny.

Kicking back the sheets, I sat on the edge of the bed. I pulled on my underwear, a pair of jeans and a T-shirt. I had half a hard-on and considered jerking off, but changed my mind. I went outside.

I had taken only a few steps under the stars when a noise from the back of the hotel made me hide behind a hedge of small bushes. A dark shape appeared in the parking lot. In the moonlight, I recognized Kheira; she was walking towards the highway. I heard a door slam, a motor start. Headlights flicked on, and I saw a Peugeot 404 van driving away.

I could feel my keys in the back pocket of my jeans and ran to my car. I opened the door, started the engine, and followed the van Kheira had gotten into.

I drove along, guided by the Peugeot's red brake lights. Trees whizzed by. We drove through a village. Beyond the last houses, the 404 turned left on to a steep road. I killed my headlights and followed. The van stopped in front of a small cemetery. I parked and switched off the engine. Kheira climbed down. She was followed by the driver, who was also wearing dark clothes and carried a shovel. They entered the cemetery.

I moved forward noiselessly, and saw them kneeling next to a grave. Then the man stood up and started to dig the rocky soil. The cemetery was on the rounded side of a wind-swept hill. It was very plain, its rough headstones shrouding the dead in the rags of poverty. Constant erosion was thinning the layer of dirt over the graves; the dust of the dead was coming closer to the open air, rising towards the sky; but what were a few inches compared to the infinity of that sky?

I could hardly believe my eyes: the man who had driven Kheira was digging right into a grave, and the blade of his shovel at once encountered the flesh of a body. As the Koran commands, the corpse had been buried directly in the earth, wrapped only in a shroud. The man held the body while Kheira removed the shroud. The burial must have taken place just the day before; the body was stiff but intact.

The man dropped the shroud into the hole he had dug, then filled in the grave. Then he set his shovel down and grabbed the body under the armpits. With Kheira holding the feet, they carried the body back to the van, and laid it in the back, under some canvas. Kheira climbed in; the man went back to get the shovel and put it in next to the body. They started up, turned around, and drove back towards the hotel with me following.

41

Leaving my car along the road before the turn-in to the parking lot, I ran towards the hotel. I saw two vertical shapes carrying a horizontal one. I crept closer. Kheira opened the back door, and a shaft of light from the kitchen struck the body lying on the ground. They carried the corpse inside the kitchen.

Bent over, I raced to a window in time to see the man lay the body on the floor. From a mat, Kheira picked up a large bowl filled with semolina. She stirred the grain, rolling it between her fingers. Then she set the bowl on the floor near the body. The man propped up the corpse a little, and Kheira moved the bowl still closer.

Using the corpse's hands, Kheira then started to stir the grains of the couscous we were to eat that noon. As the semolina trickled between the stiff fingers, Kheira softly recited a series of incantations in which the name Patrick Thévenet often recurred.

Suddenly, she turned her head towards the window where I stood watching; she had sensed my presence. I ran off and hid for a long time behind the hedge. I didn't think she had had time to recognize me.

Kheira and the man loaded the corpse back into the van under the canvas. They drove off toward the cemetery, certainly to rebury the body in its grave.

I returned to my room, undressed, and stretched out on the bed. Fortunately, it wasn't yet dawn. For her to do what she did, Kheira also needed complete darkness, before the start of the day began to dilute it.

Just before falling asleep, I suddenly realized that as they drove back toward the cemetery, Kheira and the man must have seen my car parked at the side of the road. So they knew.

I fell asleep and dreamed. When I awoke, I remembered images of the hill men of the Rif, who, after lengthy preparation, go into a trance and eat hot coals or entire cactuses. Not that they found pain divine, as I did when my torturers of the night tightened the cords cutting into my body against the concrete pillars; it was that for them pain did not exist.

I ate breakfast in the dining room. Madame Thévenet served me. Her son was still asleep. Would I be there for couscous at noon? she asked. I said I would.

A table had been laid directly under the stuffed boar's head. Five places had been set: for Madame Thévenet, her son, Mustapha, Kheira and me. Patrick Thévenet and I were the only ones to drink an aperitif.

Madame Thévenet asked us to sit down. Kheira brought out a pastilla, then served the couscous. Since I was the guest, the handle of the big wooden spoon stuck in the couscous was turned towards me. I took it without hesitation, but before I poured its contents on to my plate, I looked at Kheira. Her eyes shot me a challenge, and I sent her back one of my own. But our looks and our challenges were different; hers spoke of a death that was certain, but not mine; mine of a death that was probable, but certainly mine.

After helping myself to the couscous, I turned to look at Madame Thévenet. She had seen our exchange of glances. I thought she understood, she knew, but that she accepted in silence.

As we ate the couscous, Thévenet started to cough. His

cough became hoarse, then stopped. He said he had a stomach ache, that the pain was quickly getting very bad. He bent over, screaming that the pain was unbearable: some disgusting thing was inside him tearing at his guts, chewing through his stomach and his intestines as if it wanted to rip its way out through his belly.

Madame Thévenet went to call a doctor, but I could see in Kheira's eyes that she knew it was no use; it was too late.

Thévenet fell off his chair on to the floor, flailing around and screaming. A puddle of urine and excrement soaked through his pants and spread on the tiled floor; a stench of decay filled the room. Then he stopped thrashing and stiffened. Thévenet was dead.

The doctor came in as Kheira was mopping the floor where Thévenet had voided himself. We had laid the body out on a table. The doctor examined him, said he was baffled; it looked like poisoning, but more powerful than he had ever seen. He called the police and a Casablanca hospital, asking them to come pick up the body.

Sitting in the dining room, we waited for the police to come. Mustapha was trying to console Madame Thévenet, but for what? She hadn't cried over her son, and was behaving as if his disgusting death had been inevitable, and was perfectly normal. She was staring fixedly at the boar's head hanging on the wall. 'Mustapha,' she said, 'please throw that trash in the garbage.' The boy glanced at the hunting trophy. 'I can't touch that,' he said.

'Yes, you can. Do it for me. I don't want there to be anything left.'

Climbing on to a chair, Mustapha took the trophy down and went into the kitchen. We could hear the head dropping into the garbage can, immediately followed by the sound of Mustapha throwing up, his vomit splattering the hairs of the stuffed head.

That evening, I packed my things and left my room. I paid my bill and said goodbye to Madame Thévenet. 'What will you do now?' I asked.

'I still have some time. When Mustapha leaves, it will be all over.'

I walked to my car, opened the door, threw my bag in the back, and got in. I was about to start the engine when a face appeared at the window. It was Kheira. I rolled the window down and said, 'I won't say anything.'

'I know you won't say anything,' she said in perfect, colloquial French. 'But I have some things to say to you.'

She walked around the car, opened the passenger door, and got in next to me. 'You can probably guess what killed Patrick Thévenet,' she said. 'You don't understand, but you know that I did something to make him die. Last year, his father died the same way. I swore that the man and his descendants would disappear. It's done.'

'What about his wife?'

'That's different. I love her, and at her age, she won't have any more children. She is the opposite of everything that Roland and Patrick Thévenet stood for. Now I'm going to tell you why they died.

'Two years ago, I was living in Aïn-Sebaa, one of Casablanca's eastern districts. I had a twenty-year-old son, Mounir; he was my only child. For the previous few months, a French company had been trying to build a phosphate processing plant where our neighborhood was. They wanted to move us out. That's when Roland Thévenet showed up. The Laughing Boar had never been anything more than a front. Roland Thévenet had been here under French rule, but stayed on good terms with the new Moroccan government; he served as a middleman in their property and drug deals. So they asked him to handle the Aïn-Sebaa problem. The government needed a pretext for dispossessing the people living there; Thévenet created one. He hired agitators to incite the people to increasingly violent demonstrations. Mounir could see what was happening; he had an inborn sense of politics. We didn't have any money, but he had managed to stay on at school and go to college. He wanted to blow the whole thing wide open, of course, but he knew that something was wrong in the neighborhood, and that it would end badly. He talked to the people, and his influence on them started to grow. So Roland Thévenet got a simple idea: he had Mounir kidnapped one night, tortured and killed. They found him the next morning at the edge of the neighborhood, with his genitals stuffed in his mouth. It was a symbol borrowed from the Algerian war, and everyone got the point. The agitators started the rumor that Mounir had been a traitor, that he had been paid by French businessmen to appease the local people.

At that, the demonstrations started up again, and were much more violent than before. The army moved in two days later. Soldiers surrounded the area and opened fire with heavy machine guns. About thirty people were killed – none of the agitators, of course. The whole place was leveled and the residents evacuated. Construction on the French plant began a few months later.'

'How did you learn all this?'

'Madame Thévenet came to me after Mounir was killed. She knew what had happened, and she told me everything. She asked me to come and work at the Laughing Boar. And I've taken my revenge. Thévenet is dead, and his descendants have died with him.'

'Does she know how you caused her husband and her son's deaths?'

'I haven't told her anything, but she suspects. I know things you can't understand, and she can't either. She will never do anything to hurt me. She thinks it was fate. Maktub.'

'Because she loves Mustapha?'

'That's a sign. Your being here, your seeing me prepare the couscous, and my telling you everything is also a sign. You are here because of a woman, or rather a girl. Not for her, directly, but because of her, through a series of events. You feel that events are isolated and independent of each other, but I see links between them that you don't.'

'Laura?'

'I don't know her name, but you can't be mistaken; it can only be her. She has the face of a child. She has crossed your path several times; now she is going to become part of your life. She will have power over you, the power of a love without limits. She will hurt you, but will always make you go further. You will be followed by Arab blood, by that image of my son Mounir, with his castrated genitals in his mouth. You have been looking for something to live for. This is it.'

'I'm ill.'

'That isn't important. What is written isn't your death, but the nearness of your death, and its growing weight on you.'

I drove to Casablanca, caught a plane, and landed at Orly under an overcast sky. I bought a newspaper and learned that Jean Genet had died the night before.

I remember a phrase of his that had stuck in my mind: 'The Panthers won thanks to poetry.' He had liked the Black Panthers. They were the knife, he had said; America was the butter.

I read that Genet had been born on 19 December 1910. I was born on 19 December 1957. I didn't take the coincidence to suggest that I had any particular talent. But on the other hand, I told myself that, like him, I would have to start taking action some day – light a fuse, unpin a hand grenade, pull a submachine-gun trigger. I was intoxicated by something else that Genet, with his delighted bulldog face, had said: 'Only violence can put an end to a man's brutality.'

I called Laura from the airport, and her mother answered; Laura was living with her. When she came to the phone, I thanked her for tipping me off about the Morocco film job and asked her to have lunch with me a few days later.

Back at my place, I listened to the messages on my answering machine. Sammy had just called. I called him back.

I went to pick him up that evening at rugby practice. In the darkened city, the stadium in Pantin was a pool of light filled with boys' powerful thighs sinking their studs into the green flesh of the turf, shouts, and gusts of mist where the players' breath hit the chill night air.

Afterwards, the boys stood around the locker room

between the benches and the showers, pretending not to notice that they were being watched, penises swinging, muscles on display. I only had eyes for Sammy.

The stadium belonged to a police sports club, and the coaches were tall young policemen with mustaches and loud, confident voices and south-western accents.

As the players were getting dressed, a coach asked who wanted to come with him to André's place. The boys hesitated, both eager and afraid. Sammy said no, gesturing towards me with his chin. 'I'm eating with my friend here.'

Three of the boys accepted. They got into an unmarked Renault R18 with two of the policemen and drove out of the stadium.

As we headed towards Paris, I asked Sammy, 'What's this André business?'

'It's a cop hangout where André throws fuck parties. I hear it's well worth a visit.'

*   *   *

We had a date to meet at a café on the rue Blomet, the old Bal Nègre. I was a bit late; Laura was waiting for me at the bar, leaning against the counter. Our smiles met as I opened the glass door. We chose a table across from the pool room, beneath a first-floor balcony that ran around the room.

We sat facing each other and ordered salads. I don't remember much about the lunch except some details of our clothes and their colors. I was wearing a short, tight pair of frayed jeans, a burgundy-colored belt, and a gray-

49

and-black striped T-shirt; she had bracelets on. I got up to go to the bathroom; her eyes were on the salads. When I came back, she was looking at me; first at my face, then her eyes moved lower, stopping at my crotch.

This time, Laura troubled me less than before, and she, in turn, was more at ease. She was soft, adolescent, appealing. Wanting her, I was wanting a young girl, almost a kid, and not some mystery or vague image deep in my memory, always mixed with images of night or death.

We walked out on to the pavement. She asked me about the blue bag I was carrying. 'I'm going to go and get some exercise,' I said. I insisted on taking her home on my motorcycle, even though she lived a hundred yards from the café; we talked about this and that to delay the moment of parting.

*   *   *

During the next two months I was always the one to call her up. We would meet in the afternoon or evening and go for a walk around Paris. It reminded me of being with my first girlfriend, a friend of my cousin's in Fontainebleau. I was fifteen at the time, and still a virgin. I'd ride over with Marc on a scooter. He was going out with my cousin, and I was seeing this girl, Laurence. I didn't make love to her.

I was ten years older than Laura, but we were flirting like kids. Except that when we looked at each other, our glances sometimes went right through our clothes, making out the exact shapes of our bodies.

50

Sammy came to stay the night at my place from time to time. We jerked each other off; I would give him a blow job, and sometimes he would suck me off. He would come in my mouth, and I'd spit his cum into the sink. When I switched on the bathroom light and looked in the mirror, I no longer saw the pale face of a depressed Parisian hooked on sex like a junkie on dope; the light reflected from the orange walls gave me a golden glow. But the purple patch on my left arm continued to grow. I refused to believe it.

We didn't fuck, but it was more from lack of desire than because I had told Sammy I was HIV-positive and that we had to be careful. He didn't seem to give a damn.

Sammy was bored stiff with his job at the Bastille opera, filling out index cards and filing photos, and wanted to work at something else. So I took him on as an assistant for a job shooting a video piece on a group of students who were doing historic preservation in the Pyrenees. We flew to Perpignan, then drove to Villefranche-de-Conflent. I shot the youngsters, who spent their time potholing and restoring ruined chapels. In the mountains one day at noon, Sammy disappeared. I found him hanging in space, rock-climbing on a cliff. 'You're completely out of your mind!' I yelled. But looking at his bulging biceps and his fingers gripping the rock, I felt such a rush of desire for him, I got an instant hard-on.

*　　*　　*

It was the end of June, the evening of the big summer music festival. Laura had rung me up the night before. She knew the Taxi-Girl musicians and suggested we go hear them at the place de la Nation.

First we stopped at a café at Les Halles where the Minister of Culture was throwing a bash. 'Have you lightened your hair?' I asked Laura. She was wearing jeans, black lizard-skin boots, a long-sleeved green T-shirt and a bone bracelet. Her hair was done up in a braid.

We went backstage at la Nation. The group's bass player wasn't there, and Darc and Mirwais were playing without him. I mainly looked at Laura, who was sitting on a movable metal barrier. We're going to make love, I found myself thinking.

We were on my motorcycle, driving on the beltway towards the Porte de la Villette. Laura was cold; she had wrapped her arms around my stomach and sat huddled against my back. We spent some time at the Zénith watching has-been singers lip-syncing to records, then went to an African restaurant on the rue de la Tiquetonne for lemon chicken. As I was taking off my shoes, I said, 'I like guys, too, you know.'

We spent quite a while sitting on a bench opposite a large mural painted on a wall; splotches of color covered the cracked gray stone.

'I want to go to your place,' she said.

'It's pretty small, and not much to look at. Sure you don't mind?'

I put on an old Cure record – *Seventeen Seconds*, I think –

and we caressed each other on the bed. I sucked the tips of her breasts while she rubbed my cock through my jeans. She had a small, neat bush and a firm pussy. She unbuttoned my fly, tried to pull my jeans off; they were so tight she couldn't do it alone, and I had to help her. Then I took off my pants. I hadn't been so excited in ages. Laura slid down my chest, took my cock in her mouth, and sucked it as if she really enjoyed it.

I was going to fuck this girl. She was seventeen, I liked her, felt good with her. I found myself remembering feelings I had had as a teenager that I'd never felt with Carol: wanting a woman. On the surface, it was simple: I could forget the boys, those I had loved, those I had only glimpsed during my savage nights, who had just given me their bodies, their sperm, or their piss. Kheira's voice came back to me, but all I remembered of her prophesies was that I would have a long relationship with Laura. I couldn't risk ruining that before it could even begin. In any case, I didn't have any condoms at home, and found I couldn't admit to her I was HIV-positive.

So I rolled Laura over on her back, and moved on to her; she guided my cock in. We made love for a long time; I couldn't believe how good it felt. She came with a scream, clawing at my back. I fucked her again, then came with a throaty yell, feeling I was coming as I'd never come before.

Rolling on to my side, I realized I didn't have that sick feeling, gray and acid, that I used to get after an orgasm with Carol. I was floating, knowing that I had shot her full of sperm that was infected with a deadly virus, but feeling that it was all right, that nothing would happen, because we were starting what could truly be called a 'love story'.

Next morning, I got up and pulled on a University of California T-shirt, kimono pants, and a pair of slippers. This made Laura laugh. She must have been wondering, 'Who is this guy, anyway?'

I had a meeting with Jaime. The three of us went to the movies to see *Runaway Train*, and ate dinner at the Hippopotamus on the Champs-Elysées. It reminded me of ten or fifteen years ago, when Marc and I used to get drunk in the Vélizy 2 or Parly 2 student canteens.

Laura called her mother, who hadn't heard from her in twenty-four hours and was worried. The talk got heated. 'Fuck off!' yelled Laura, and slammed down the receiver.

Jaime suggested we go with him to a friend's apartment to smoke joints and snort coke. I wasn't interested; I wanted to go home and fuck Laura. I asked her to come sleep at my place; she wanted to go to hers, that is, to her mother's. Finally, she said, 'All right, one last night at your place.' I didn't understand what she meant by 'one last night', but said nothing. Jaime took off by himself. I swung on to the seat of the motorcycle, and Laura nestled against me.

We made love, more slowly than the night before. I still couldn't bring myself to tell her I was HIV-positive, but just thinking about it kept me from coming, which was just as well. After she came, I jerked off on to my belly.

*   *   *

I went to see the head of Shaman Video and asked him if he

could take Sammy on. He said he'd hire him as a gofer and promised to train him as an assistant cameraman.

Sammy was living with Marianne, his journalist friend. I met her one evening when I called for him, and we eyed each other like two dogs sniffing at the same bone. I found her beautiful, especially her blue, nearly violet eyes. She had met Sammy in the métro when he was sixteen. Two days later, Serge had picked Sammy up while he and Marianne were roller-skating on the plaza of the Montparnasse tower.

Out of vanity, self-interest, and a need to seduce, Sammy had played along with Serge's little games: photos of him bare-chested in leather shorts, videos of his ass shot from every possible angle, sliding out of the sheets in a London hotel or hugged by tight-fitting jeans, pretending to mount the clinking body of a pinball machine.

I knew Marianne hated Serge; did she suspect I was sleeping with Sammy? Serge had drifted away, and now I had showed up in Sammy's life. 'Christ, can't these damned faggots leave me in peace?'

'Do you want to come with us?'

'I'm staying here,' Marianne said. 'I have work to do.' She was writing an article.

I closed the door and clattered down the stairs after Sammy. We headed for the Pacifico.

We were drinking Tecate and mescal, and Sammy was drunk. This time, I was able to get him to talk.

He had been on leave from his military service and Marianne met him on the railway platform. His hair was cropped short; he was tanned and fit, rippling with strength. She screamed with pleasure under his battering-ram thrusts. He reported to his barracks at seventeen, and the first thing the captain said to him was, 'What are your intentions in enlisting in the mountain troops?'

'Christ, what an asshole!' Sammy said. 'Here I was burying myself in the army because I didn't know what else to do, because I had a faggot on my ass, because I was breaking into apartments and knew I'd end up in trouble, and here this fucking officer wanted us to know what my "intentions" were! I was willing to fight and die. Wasn't that enough?'

All Sammy wanted was to glissade down glaciers on his heels, to let himself slide. It was a slide that had started a long time before . . . He had been nine years old, on his way home from boarding school in Cahors for the Christmas holidays. The train pulled into Toulouse railway station. He hadn't seen his parents since the summer. Soon, his father would lift him high in the air and Sammy would feel the strong grip on his arms, imagine the muscles bulging under his father's shirt. He got up from the bench; a guy helped him get his things down from the luggage-rack. His chest prickled in the cold, humid air; he snapped his jacket closed. But Sammy felt afraid: a draught of black air had swept across the pink town. His father wasn't standing at the foot of the carriage's steps; neither was his mother. Only his sister was there, alone. Her face was hard but her eyes were moist. 'Why didn't dad come?' he asked. She didn't know what to say. 'He couldn't; he had to work today.'

'What about mom?'

'She couldn't either.'

They took a bus. It started to rain; behind the vertical streaks of the droplets on the windows, Sammy was aware of other streaks, horizontal ones, snatches of building façades like strokes of pink gouache on a canvas. He was cold. He felt frightened and started to cry. Then Lydia put her arm around his neck and pulled him tightly against her. She was four years older and smelled of vanilla. She looked him straight in the eye and said, 'The cops came to arrest dad at home this morning.'

'I tell you, I started to weigh a lot then. I thought that later, when I was eighteen or twenty, the age I am now, I would weigh a lot, too. But it would be the weight of muscles, like my dad's, not the weight of sorrow.'

In the bus that was taking them home, Lydia and Sammy weren't talking any more. She hugged him, and he could feel her small, firm breasts against his cheek. Then she started to tell him about their father's arrest. She had been asleep; her mother's screams woke her. She ran to their room, stopped on the threshold. The cops had broken down the door, ripped the sheets from the bed, dragged dad across the bedroom floor. Mom had covered herself with a sheet and was standing there, screaming and swearing in Spanish. The father had got an erection in his sleep. A young cop saw his stiff cock, and cracked up. 'No little morning quickie for you, nigger!' Lydia had started shaking convulsively. Later, she drank some coffee with milk and vomited it into the toilet bowl.

'Lydia was supposed to keep quiet, see, but she knew I could understand, so she told me everything. My mom came home that evening; I was watching TV. I remember I was stretched out on the sofa, with my head in Lydia's lap. She came over and kissed me, and said, "Dad won't be home during the holidays; he's found a new job in electronics, and he'll be traveling in the north of France until January." I glanced at Lydia, smiled, and said, "Is it a good job? Is the pay good?" A little later, during dinner, I

57

said, "Shit, dad should be here, I'm at home for once!" '

The Pacifico was jammed, echoing with laughter, caresses, declarations of love, and dirty jokes in French, English and Spanish. We drank a few more Tecates and I questioned Sammy about his father, but he didn't want to tell me anything further; not even which of the Magreb countries he came from.

I left him in front of the block where Marianne lived. Their bodies would touch; that hurt. Yet it could all have been so simple: I had Laura, the outline of a love.

To fight the pain, I had to descend to the humiliation whose help I regularly sought. Under the Grenelle bridge, in Swan Alley, no light brightens the night. The shapes that come together there are human, unless they belong to black swans, Australian swans.
   A boy with a shaved skull wearing army surplus pants and combat boots pressed me against one of the bridge abutments, pushed his knee into my balls. On the far bank, the Maison de la Radio blazed with light when the guy moved his head out of the way. He spat on my lips. I pissed in his hands, and he smeared the piss on my face. No memories.

*   *   *

But I returned to Laura pure. I could have gone to the same sexual extremes with her that I did during those nights, and nothing would have changed. Mud, spit, piss, sperm and shit can all be washed off with soap and water.

I liked having her breasts against my chest, my cock in her twat. I didn't kiss her often or explore her body. Sammy was the one I liked to caress, the one I wanted to kiss, but he preferred women.

I loved Laura, loved Sammy, loved the vices of my savage nights. Was I born so completely divided? Or had I been cut into pieces, little by little, because I would have been too dangerous unified, too uncontrollable?

I was a coward. I thought I was coming to Laura washed of the stains from my nights, while silently exposing her to the corruption of my blood. I was shooting my virus into her and saying nothing. My silence haunted me.

When I wanted to tell her, I couldn't. She had just turned eighteen; all I could see was abused innocence, a life shot to hell.

*   *   *

The film I had written with Omar was being shown at the Swiss cultural center, to be followed by a question-and-answer session. Omar's wife had just given birth to a little girl; he was at her bedside, and had asked me to go to the discussion in his place.

I took Sammy. We laughed and talked before the lights in the auditorium went down. A girl sitting a few rows ahead of us kept turning around and smiling at us. Sammy found her attractive. After the screening and the discussion, I ran into her in the street. Sammy, suddenly shy, came over. She was Swiss, she said, from Lausanne; her name was Sylvie. She was in Paris to study drawing.

She had a room in the Cité des Arts, but usually slept at

a girlfriend's place. It was empty that night, so she took us there. Two large rooms; mattresses on the floor; dirty dishes stacked on a kind of counter next to the kitchen with a dish of cold spaghetti in tomato sauce; drawings and canvases hung on the walls or piled on the floor.

We caressed Sylvie together. Occasionally, my hands continued beyond her body to touch Sammy's, and in turn let his hands play on me. Our caresses startled her. Sammy, to provoke her, said, 'He's my man!' I played along but I sensed that Sylvie wanted to make love with only one of us, and hadn't yet decided which one. And while caressing me, Sammy was pushing me away from her. Because he knew that I desired him more than I did her; by exciting me he drew me closer to him, and further from the girl. In a few minutes, they were in each other's arms, Sammy's cock stiff against her body, with me lying off to one side.

I went into the next room and lay down. The mess, the mattresses on the floor, and the filth reminded me of the early eighties . . . I'd just come back from Puerto Rico, tanned and drunk on sex and sunshine. Riding in a taxi through the French grayness that lay over Paris, I still reeked of the three lovers that I had had the night before: Edson, who drove Joe the lawyer's Cadillac without a licence and sold Quaaludes in the Santulce slums; Max, who swindled tourists on Condado Avenue; and Orlando – sweet, gentle Orlando with his mustache – to whom I gave myself just because he had wanted to make love to me for days. The taxi dropped me off in front of Marc's place. I rang the doorbell of the apartment he was sharing with a friend who worked as an engineer for an oil company. Marc was still in school; a few months earlier I too had been in engineering school.

Marc's flat had two rooms, mattresses on the floor, dirty laundry in a corner, balls of dust blown around by the drafts, smog greasing the edges of the windows and the outside of the glass, the lingering smell of two boys and the more ephemeral ones of visiting girls. To rediscover all those images almost ten years later in an apartment where Sammy was fucking Sylvie and I was waiting to fall asleep in the next room . . .

Marc hadn't heard from me for several months, but when he saw me standing in the doorway, it was as if we had parted just the night before. I didn't have a place to crash, so he suggested I put a mattress down in the hallway between the two rooms. I accepted, and lived there for a month or two.

One evening at the Trocadéro, I met a young guy who said he was assistant magician to Gérard Majax. I brought him back to my hallway, thinking Marc and the engineer were asleep. I unrolled the mattress, we got undressed, and the guy started to fuck me. I was screaming with pleasure when the engineer's door opened; he was bare chested, in his underwear, and had to step over us to go and piss. Coming out of the bathroom, he looked completely disgusted when he saw us. The magician fell over laughing. The engineer knocked on Marc's door, who told him to come in. I spied a towel draped over the bedside light and the back of a girl who was straddling Marc in bed. 'Am I disturbing you?' asked the engineer.

'Not at all; I'm glad you dropped by. Arlette here was just asking me at what stage you get paraffin when refining crude oil.'

'Excuse me . . .'

'Do you need something?'

'No, nothing . . . believe me, it's nothing.'

At breakfast the next day, the engineer told Marc that he was giving up the apartment, and that I might as well take his room. I asked him if it was because of the scene he had witnessed during the night. He mumbled yes, no, maybe. In any case, he'd been offered a job in Dubai. He was leaving for five years; triple salary, of which part would be deposited in a frozen bank account until he came back; it was too good to turn down . . .

I was laughing to myself when Sammy came in, but immediately put on the expression of a neglected lover. He stretched out next to me, gave me a hug and a few kisses, then got up and went back next door. He shuttled a few times between the rooms, checking on my frustration, then going back to make love to Sylvie. Or at least that's what I thought for the rest of the night; I slept badly, constantly awakened by cries of pleasure that existed only in my dreams.

Next morning, we were drinking coffee at a stand on the avenue des Gobelins. I asked Sammy if he'd spent a pleasant night. 'I went down on her,' he said, 'and she sucked me off while sticking a finger up my ass, but there was no way she was going to let me jump her!'

'If you had slept in my bed, you could have fucked me.'

*   *   *

Time seemed to be made up of two irreconcilable elements: destiny and discontinuity. I was living a story written by my past, my illness and Kheira's prophecies.

62

But I was also living many other stories: needs and desires, islands of events that were totally unconnected.

Laura was lying on her back, and I was pressing down on her. 'I've been with a lot of boys, you know,' I said. 'And they weren't always saints; some were ten-minute quickies.' I wanted her to understand without my having to tell her. 'I've gone with a lot of guys,' I repeated. 'Maybe I should put on a condom.' I didn't dare tell her the truth, and my cowardice disgusted me. But I had dreamed of a peaceful love for so long. I took the condom out of the package and unrolled it on to my cock.

After making love, we agreed that I wouldn't wear a condom any more. Laura wanted to feel the skin of my cock, and I wanted to feel all of her. Our lives culminated in that penetration; we weren't going to let a bit of latex mask the pleasure.

*   *   *

One Sunday I went to have lunch with Sammy at his parents' place south of the city. His mother looked after the offices of a consumer research company; his step-father, a Chilean named Paulo, took care of the gardens.

The rooms were square, with very high cement walls. A whiff of Mediterranean cooking impregnated the sofa, armchairs and rugs: they smelled of garlic, tomatoes, basil and olive oil. Sammy had lived in this cement fishbowl, had loved the house that curbed his erratic movements.

Nobody spoke of his father, but one felt his presence

everywhere: a yawning void that left Sammy ready for anything.

On the drive back to Paris, Sammy's fixed stare rested on an imaginary horizon barred by cars and apartment buildings. 'My father's still very handsome,' he said. 'He worked with Paulo for a long time. The Chilean could handle explosives better than anyone; no safe could withstand him. They were real pros who didn't piss away their time stealing three hundred francs from little old ladies in wheelchairs. They spent days planning an operation, thinking everything out.'

Sammy frightened me. His admiration was rigid and inflexible; he wasn't thinking any more. For a moment, I saw the fanatic in him. 'Was he the one who left your mother, or did she leave him?' I asked.

'They hadn't been getting on, and he got busted for a jewel robbery. He got eight years. And she ditched him.'

'So she got together with Paulo?'

'That happened later. She moved to Paris, started working in the Pigalle bars. The Chilean came to join her. It was all right for a while, and then she got sick of it. They never had any cash. She served drinks but refused to go upstairs with the customers. He was going straight; he wasn't working. So she hooked up with a Dutchman who was visiting Paris, a filthy rich butcher who used to drink from restaurant fingerbowls! We went to Amsterdam with him. I was thirteen, and got fucked by a tram conductor; I already told you that. After six months, my mother couldn't stand it any more. We came back to Paris, she took up with Paulo again, and they found the place they have now.'

We spent the afternoon and evening in the Pigalle bars, slouched on the tall stools, drinking, as girls looked us over. We didn't talk much. 'With any luck,' Sammy said, 'we'll run into one of my mother's girlfriends who used to bounce me on her knee!'

Then, later: 'How old were you when you first slept with a girl?'

'Seventeen. I wasn't precocious.'

'And a guy?'

'Twenty-one.'

'Me, I lost it to one of my mother's friends. She came over to babysit me and my sister, and when Lydia fell asleep, she came into my room and taught me about making love. She was the wife of the guy who counterfeited two-hundred-franc notes just before the real ones came out.'

*   *   *

With Laura, I found myself talking less. I'd been asked to shoot a film about African musicians living in Paris, so I hired her to gather information on them. But then the government changed; 'cultural assimilation' wasn't fashionable any more, and the project was abandoned.

When we were together, we didn't spend time on words or caresses, they led straight to orgasm. We took a trip to Lyons. Rashid, a singer with Carte de Séjour,* had asked me to participate in an evening fundraiser for two hunger

* Carte de séjour - green card. (*Tr.*)

65

strikers who opposed the new nationality law. Laura bought me a little stuffed dog called Hassan Cehef!* at the railroad station, and sucked me off in the toilet on the train. At La Part-Dieu, we went looking for an open restaurant. It was a Sunday evening, and the business districts we crossed were empty. I was in constant pain: the night before, my dentist had put in four false teeth. The same blood that stiffened my cock to penetrate Laura was pounding in my gums, still sore from the electric needle.

* * *

The doctor examined the purple patch on my left arm. 'It doesn't look like anything, but we'll do a biopsy just the same. You never know.'

I was lying on an examination table at Tarnier Hospital. A syringe filled with local anaesthetic in her hand, the dermatologist lifted my arm and made a few injections around the purple patch, then two cuts around the lesion with a scalpel. She pulled off the patch of skin, put in a couple of stitches, and bandaged the wound.

'We'll analyse the biopsy specimen,' she said. 'You'll have the results in a few days.'

* * *

* A play on 'SNCF', the initials of the French national railway. (*Tr.*)

Night was falling, and an orange halo crowned the Meudon hill. A south-westerly breeze was blowing from the municipal garbage incinerators, carrying a nauseating smell of garlic and vanilla to my windows. I had a lot of cocaine in my blood. I was waiting for Laura. Iggy Pop was singing 'Real Wild Child'. I was excited; cocaine increases desire but delays orgasm; I was going to fuck Laura until I rubbed her raw and the pain turned into pleasure. Watching myself in the bathroom mirror, I stroked my cock through the fly of my tight, ragged jeans.

I turned on the TV and caught the news. A prison guard had been struck by lightning seven times. His hair had caught fire; his eyebrows and a big toe had gone up in smoke. That was it: my sickness was a jail without guards. Genet came to mind. Sickness is my prison, I thought to myself, my personal Devil's Island. A parallel world that defies the society that exists on the front pages of newspapers but sometimes collides with it, when blood and sperm spin an aerial bridge between them. Love must penetrate the walls of the cells. During exercise periods, the merest glance, the slightest physical contact, become what they are on the outside: a feverish declaration of love followed by a beautiful, clear orgasm. Under those malevolent tropics, the most hardened murderer would wait for the chosen child to show his love in the trembling of his body. Without making a move, he could desire the kid to the point of tears, or else take everything by force: his asshole, his fresh lips and his youthful years.

As for me, I was waiting for Laura. Love had entered my prison, too. I could no longer lie or ignore the wound I was carrying.

She rang the doorbell, and I let her in. We kissed. Walking down the hallway in front of her, I heard her say,

'Those jeans look good on you; they make your ass look great.' I turned round and came close to her. She looked down, and said, 'This side isn't bad either!' I stroked her breasts through a tan sweater, cupped her ass with my hands, pressed my crotch against hers. 'Laura, I've taken the AIDS test,' I said. 'I'm HIV-positive.'

She swallows the revolting thing my words have made. She doesn't budge as it enters her, neither retreat nor abandonment. We're going to make love. I put a condom on my cock; Laura rips it off and throws it into an ashtray. But from then on, I don't ever come inside her again.

*　　*　　*

Laura is alone at her mother's. Sobbing in her bed, she can't get to sleep. She calls a girlfriend who drops by with some video cassettes. Huddled together, they watch *A Streetcar Named Desire*.
　　'I was afraid for you,' she tells me the next day, 'not for me.' But the sobs return; she's drowning in her tears. When she calms down a bit, she says, 'I couldn't help remembering what happened to me with Frank. I was crazy about him. He had gone to the United States; I was sixteen. One night he called me at two in the morning, said that he was back in Paris, that he was coming to get me in ten minutes. I got dressed, had a fight with my mom, who didn't want me to go out. Frank was downstairs in a BMW convertible. It was summer; we drove around the beltway at top speed, and then somehow wound up in a maid's room in Boulogne. I wanted him, so we got undressed, and I started to suck him off. I don't know what

happened, but I somehow nipped his cock with my teeth. The blood started to flow, it filled my mouth, got all over my face, started dripping down my belly. We went to the little bathroom, and Frank started washing his cock in the pale light. But it kept on bleeding, and suddenly he turned towards me and said, "I've got AIDS." And I believed him, I thought he must have caught it in the United States, and that's why he was bleeding like that, that he'd become a hemophiliac or something . . . I looked at myself in the mirror, covered with blood, and I started screaming and crying, I couldn't stop. And he told me, "It isn't true, I don't have AIDS. Christ, you've gone crazy!" But I kept on screaming. I asked him to take me home, and then I couldn't sleep for the rest of the night, thinking I was fucked, that I was going to die, and I couldn't stop crying. Next day, I told my mother everything.'

Laura looks at me and says, 'To think that since you told me you're HIV-positive I've only been afraid for you. I'm not even thinking of myself.'

*   *   *

I called the hospital for the biopsy results, and asked for the doctor. 'I've just come from the lab,' he said. 'They weren't quite sure, so I had a look myself. There's a good chance that it's a Kaposi's sarcoma caused by the virus.'

Sammy is at my place. We snort some coke, then I go and pick up Laura, who is waiting downstairs at her mother's with her suitcase. Tomorrow, we're flying to Corsica. Carol calls while I'm out, and Sammy says, 'He went to pick up his girlfriend.'

I return with Laura, and we do some more coke. She

and Sammy are fooling around. He puts a Bérurier Noir record on the turntable and turns the volume all the way up. 'Oh, unlucky fox, the soldiers have seen you . . . Oh, unlucky fox, your rage is hardly lost . . .'

Sammy starts to sing along with the record at the top of his lungs. When he can't remember the lyrics, he yells, 'This is for the Apaches of Tokoyo, the Mohicans of Paris and the Redskins of Dijon.' Then he suddenly remembers. 'Shit, I forgot to tell you; Carol called.'

I get angry. 'Christ, couldn't you have told her something besides, "He went to pick up his girlfriend"?'

Later, Sammy announces that he's leaving. 'I'll console Carol a bit; I'm going to go down on her!' I approve, half-awake: 'You're right, she's the clitoral type. Laura's vaginal; if you want to console her, you give her your cock, nice and deep.' Laura says, 'Refined, aren't you?' but only as a joke. Sex talk doesn't shock her.

A few weeks before, Sammy, Carol and I had done a threesome together, and he's been seeing her ever since. I told him I didn't care to play that game; it had already caused me enough pain. But that was just a pretext. The fact is, I no longer desire Carol; thinking of her reminds me of having an octopus caress me with its sticky tentacles.

Sammy picks up his helmet. 'You have a motorcycle, now?' I say. 'Where did you steal it from?'

'None of your business! I'm working these days. I'm an honest wage-earner.'

Sammy has left. We go to stay at my parents' place in Versailles, in the little upstairs room under the eaves. I

fuck Laura, but I have so much coke in my system I can't
fall asleep despite my orgasm. I take a Seconal and two
Nembutals. The bed is very narrow. Sleep finally comes.

* * *

Our Fokker lands at the Figari airport. Michel meets us
and takes us to Porto-Vecchio. He's still a mailman and
is free after making his morning rounds. His wife looks
after the estate of a millionaire from the mainland; she's
breeding German shepherds, trained to attack. Every day,
Michel practices shooting at cans with a Magnum .357.
One of these days, he's going to bump off some Dutch
tourist who's pitched his tent on the estate. We cross the
'village of the Downs', where all the inhabitants look
Mongoloid because of inbreeding. He drops us off at the
harbor. We climb aboard the yacht I've been lent, a brand-
new thirty-five-footer.

The next few days are quiet ones, as if we were passing
through the eye of a hurricane. We sail, our skin turns
brown in the sun. Laura is beautiful. We make love: I take
her seated on the steps of the companionway, her
miniskirt pushed up, underwear torn off. The salt water
irritates the sore on my left arm, but I begin to forget the
hospital's smell of ether, the ranker smell of my savage
nights, even the smell of Sammy's body.

* * *

71

At Saint Raphael, we split up: I'm heading back to Paris, Laura is stopping over at Saint-Tropez. She takes the boat across the bay, crying in the darkness under the stars.

I call her up from Paris: 'I miss you,' I say. 'I want you.' I call Sammy; Marianne tells me he's gone mountain climbing until the end of the month. I call Laura back.

But it's August and Paris is on vacation. The city's warm innards, full of half-glimpsed, intertwined bodies, are free for the taking. I pull on a pair of jeans, a sweater and a jacket and join the tangle of bodies.

I meet a big brown guy with a crewcut, wearing leather pants. Without a word, our hands go straight for our crotches. He shoves me against a cement pillar, pushes me to my knees, forces my mouth against his cock, stiff under the leather. I slide down along his legs, roll in the dust. He presses the heel of his boot on my thighs, my chest, my crotch. I pull out my cock and jerk off in the dust I've raised, writhing with pleasure, and come on to my belly. Standing over me, he comes, and his sperm drips on to my face and hair. He walks away, fading into the shadows. I stand up and walk along the quay towards the upper world.

Laura drives back from Saint-Tropez with a guy with a silly smile, an advertising model type. I can't find out whether they slept together. She deliberately leaves the question open.

I have dinner with her in a brasserie on the avenue de la Motte-Picquet. Our legs touch under the table, I caress her breasts through her T-shirt; at the neighboring tables, heads swivel towards us. She closes her eyes, strokes her temple, opens them again. Desire surrounds us like a damp halo. She asks for the bill and we leave, headed for love.

Three days later, Laura has an appointment in an office on the Champs-Elysées and runs into a guy who once picked her and her mother up one evening in a Saint-Tropez restaurant. They stop at the guy's apartment on the avenue Foch to get his things, then take off from Le Bourget in his private plane and fly south. Laura's mother meets them at Saint-Tropez airport.

*　　*　　*

Sammy is back in Paris and calls me up. We get together at Jaime's, snort coke and drink J&B. Sammy tells me he went to see his father in Toulouse. 'He's working for an electronics company now. We went for a drive in his boss's Porsche!'

Jaime launches into his favorite theme, and I follow the rest of the conversation in silence. 'A rebel is marked by fate, and his dignity is inside him. Your father's like all the other losers, he thinks that it's what's on the outside that makes you respectable, so he makes gestures that don't mean anything.'

'An' I s'pose you're the kind of highwayman who robs from the rich to give to the poor.'

'There aren't anything but highways left!'

'Those were the good old days . . . And jus' imagine making love, getting through all those petticoats.'

'With a lock on the chastity belt because her guy's gone off on the Crusades . . .'

'If he dies over there, imagine the poor girl . . . Think she could give herself a finger, at least?'

'Through the keyhole!'

'See, Jaime, now that I'm working, I'm proving something to my father. I told him, "Dad, I'm working in video." And he didn't call me a jerk-off, or make me feel lower than a worm, the way he usually does.'

'And what did he prove, with his break-ins and his eight years in the pen?'

'He didn't get caught, they ratted on him. Anyway, it's just for show; it's talk, all talk.'

'An' all for money. Money, always money!'

'I've always been around people who didn't have any, and wanted it. My mom always paid her debts, even if we had to eat nothing but noodles . . . I'm proud I was able to lend him three thousand francs last month.'

'You owe your father one debt I hope you'll never repay.'

'What's that?'

'He's sticking his damned ideas into your head!'

*　　*　　*

Laura's found a job selling expensive clothes in a boutique on the place des Victoires, but it doesn't last: the manager can't stand watching her serving customers while chewing gum.

She calls me: 'I've been fired and my mother doesn't

want me living with her. She's kicking me out tomorrow morning.'

I've never been very good at responding to other people's complaints, and I'm getting worse. The evidence of other's failures leaves me feeling hard-hearted. Instead of being sympathetic, I tell her I'm not surprised she isn't able to hold on to a job: 'When you were gathering information on African musicians for me, you did the work of three people for a few days, then suddenly got fed up and fucked off. How do you expect someone who hires you to understand that sort of thing?' She starts to cry. 'I'm being thrown out into the street, and you don't give a damn.'

I can't stand tears; they disgust me. Especially girls' tears, which are so conventional and predictable. At most, a boy's tears, if they're paradoxical, can still move me. I hang up.

Laura calls back. The tears are still there, but they're held back now, almost forgotten. 'Fine birthday present this is!' she says. 'No more job, my mom's throwing me out, and my boyfriend's HIV-positive and didn't tell me and may have given me that shit. Fuck, do you realize I'm only eighteen? I'm just a kid! You're ten years older than I am. You have no right to use that to hurt me.'

I try to say something nice, but the words come out with difficulty. My lips barely move, colliding with a smooth wall that's been in place too long for Laura's unhappiness to destroy it. I tell her to come and stay at my place tomorrow night.

As soon as I hang up, I feel sick. I'm disgusted at myself. I'm like some rusted-up machine, able to feel only my own pain. And even that has to be artificially created, according to the rituals I associate with pleasure. I slip on a jacket and go out.

I'm driving through Paris, holding my video camera in my left hand and steering with my right. The city and the night blur into a series of lateral pans, broken only by the red lights at intersections.

A couple is fighting on the central reservation on avenue René-Coty. The man grabs the woman by the shoulders, shoves her backwards; she hangs on to him, screaming. He pushes her again and she falls back. The man walks on alone, she catches up with him, hits him in the back with her handbag. He turns around, grabs the woman's arm, whirls her around and lets go. She tumbles to the pavement, twists her wrist trying to break her fall, grazes her knee. I stop filming, get out of my car, walk over to her.
    'What's going on?'
    'It's nothing. Leave me alone.'
    'Is he giving you a hard time?'
    'Stop bothering me! Fuck off!'
    She sees the man walking away so she gets up, looks at her knee, walks after him, limping a little. She calls to him, but without shouting; he stops; she's hardly crying, says a few words in a hoarse voice, comes slowly closer to him, as if expecting to be hit. She doesn't get quite near enough to touch him. He starts off again; she walks alongside him; she turns to look at him, he's staring straight ahead, the horizon of stupidity.
    They're both trashed. I film their backs as they melt into the night's vague darkness, colored orange and green by the glow of street-lights filtered through the leaves of the trees.

Place d'Italie; boulevard Vincent-Auriol; the elevated métro. I walk down towards the river, the concrete, the smell of urine at summer's end.

Hands unbutton my fly, pull up my T-shirt, pinch and twist my nipples. The extension of these hands torturing my chest is a man's body. This pain belongs to me; it's a necessary evil.

I pull the man towards an area lit by a ray of light shining down from the street through an air vent, projecting a grillwork pattern on to the wall. We're going to come in an imaginary cage, a cell with bars made of nothing but light and shadow.

I'm not pulling the man towards this brighter area to see his face, or see if he's handsome or ugly, smooth or scarred by sickness, but so my own body can be seen. I'm an exhibitionist, but above all I'm my own voyeur.

The man's wearing rubber pants and his skin is soaked. Under his pincerlike hands and sawtooth mouth, the skin of my nipples splits and a few red drops flow. Pearls of blood, precious pearls.

*　　*　　*

Laura's been living at my place since her mother kicked her out. She's enrolled in film school; the classes are expensive, but her grandparents in Cannes have agreed to pay for them. Two weeks of calm, living in the same room with a girl: I wouldn't have thought it possible. I tell her how amazed I am. With her around, I'm not as afraid; I feel good; I often forget the threat of illness.

Laura strikes me as strong; she doesn't mention her fear that I may have infected her. I like her tastes, her opinions, what she has to say about a film or a song. She seems all the stronger because I've never felt so weak.

Laura's in the bathroom. The phone rings, and I answer. It's Olivier; can we get together? he wants to know. We make a date for that evening. For the last four years, Olivier has been calling me up once or twice a month; I take him out to dinner, we come back to my place and sleep together.

I first met Olivier when he was sixteen, living in a reform school in Ivry, and I was working on a short film about the boys of the house. It was my first film as chief cameraman. After the first take, I was shaking. I sat down on a bench muttering over and over again, 'Shit, I fucked up, I'm not cut out for this kind of work . . .'

Olivier had a part in the film. He was crazy about photography and was forever hanging around the camera watching me work. When the shoot was over, he asked if he could see me again so I could advise him on how to become a photographer's assistant. I gave him my phone number.

He phoned a week later and came over. I was sharing the apartment with Marc. Olivier didn't want to go back to the reform school, and asked if he could sleep there. My room only had one bed. He undressed and got into it.

His parents were Arabs, but he'd been brought up by farmers in Burgundy. He thought of me as his big brother. He would call me at regular intervals, and come over. We slept together, but nothing happened. I waited for him to make the first move.

Three years later, he snuggled into my arms, with a hard-on. I stroked and sucked him. He lay still, unresisting. He jerked off and came. Only then did he dare to caress me.

Laura steps out of the bathroom. Naked, her skin still

damp, she nestles against me and I squeeze her ass with my hands. Then I realize I've told Olivier to come over and that she's here. 'What'll we do this afternoon?' she asks.

'Laura, there's a problem about tonight, you can't stay here, I've invited a friend to stay the night.'

Open-mouthed, she doesn't understand. She feels good, she's happy, and my words land between us like a bomb. She pretends: 'Put a mattress on the floor for him.'

'I don't have one, and it's not what you think.'

'I don't think anything, I'm just here, that's all.'

'Shit, this is my place, I can have anybody I like to stay, can't I?'

Livid, Laura pulls on a T-shirt and jeans, looks for her address book, calls a girlfriend: 'Can I sleep at your place? There'll be some guy in the bed here instead of me.'

Laura's gone. Tonight, Olivier will sleep next to me. Sammy calls; tomorrow, it'll be him. I'm passive. Events follow one another. I submit to them.

My head is on Olivier's belly. He's jerking off, with my mouth brushing the end of his prick. He comes on to my lips. I wipe my face and say, 'You like that, don't you?' He doesn't answer, lights a cigarette, lifts the pillow and leans back on it against the wall. 'There was a guy at Ivry, he seemed old to us, he must have been twenty, he often came to the reform school but he didn't live there. He had an awesome car, a Renault R30 V-6. Used to park it in front of the gate, and we'd all come over to check out his wheels. The guy was smuggling VCRs right under the

79

counselors' noses; he was dealing in heroin, and nobody said a word. I'm sure he gave the reform school money and that's why everybody looked the other way. He liked me, used to give me dope. I'd send it to a friend in jail by sticking it under the stamps on the envelope. This guy didn't take shit from anybody, I swear. One day when he was there, the cops wanted to raid the house. He came out, started shouting, climbed on top of their car screaming. People in the neighborhood opened their windows to see what was going on, the cops were shitting bricks, so they bugged off. The guy, his name was Mick, sometimes he'd spend the night at the house. He always slept in the room of a shy fourteen-year-old. The kid looked out of it, couldn't stand up for himself, but nobody gave him any shit because they knew Mick was protecting him. I think they were fucking.'

Next day, I'm to meet Laura at the Newstore on the Champs-Elysées. I pull up on my motorcycle; Sammy's riding behind me, his arms around my waist. Laura's there already; she spots us through the plate-glass window.

I order an Irish beer, sensing catastrophe in the air. I search for words for Laura, but can't find any. She goes on the attack: 'Spend a pleasant night?'

'Please, let's not start on that.'

'Keep your shirt on. What did I say, anyway? What the fuck did I say? You've got a real sense of humor, you know, it's a pleasure!'

I glance at Sammy. He's handsome. I think of last night; I can't stand Olivier's teeth anymore. Laura puts her hand on mine. 'Why don't you ever look at me the way you look at Sammy?' Luckily, he answers: 'You're out of your mind, Laura. He's got his hangdog look because he's got troubles, that's all.'

We're out on the pavement in front of my bike. The tension is mounting. We don't know what to do; I can't take both Laura and Sammy behind me. I took the bike instead of my car so as to force myself to choose, and now that the moment's come, I can't. I feel sick, my legs are weak, I feel terribly weary.

We're going around in circles, we don't feel like doing anything. Yet I'm the one who created this malaise. So as not to have to choose, I flee. 'I don't have any ideas and don't want to, but since you can't come up with any either, I'm going!' I pull on my helmet, climb on the bike, and start it up. I know Sammy: he's going to take advantage of the situation.

I wasn't wrong: Sammy took Laura to Marianne's; Marianne was away on an assignment in Poland. She was crying, wanted to call me all the time. Sammy told her not to. He made herb tea for her. She stretched out on the bed on the floor. He started rubbing her back and shoulders; she took off her T-shirt; he was bare chested, wearing only his pants.

Sammy's hands on Laura's gradually relaxing body. He reached around to caress her breasts. She was lying on her stomach and could feel Sammy's stiff cock in his pants brushing against her ass when he leaned against her to rub the back of her neck. Laura rolled over on to her back and Sammy pulled off her jeans, stroked her twat through the silk panties. They slipped under the sheets, he pulled her to him. She said, 'We aren't going to make love, Sammy. I don't want to, I'm sorry.'

She spent a week at Marianne's; Marianne was still in Poland. Sammy kept up the massages and the herb tea, but Laura didn't give in. When I called, she would start crying again, because I barely said hello to her but had long talks with Sammy. She felt I wanted him and that she was in the way. I came over a couple of times and didn't look at her.

Laura's telling me all this. She says that Sammy's two-faced. 'He kisses your ass when you're there and makes fun of you as soon as your back is turned.'

This is before we make love. I'm imagining Sammy excited by Laura's body which she's refusing him. She stares at my prick. 'You've got a hard-on as big as a horse,' she says with a laugh. 'I've never seen you so huge!' I penetrate her and say, 'I don't know how you managed to resist Sammy.'

'You're the one I love, that's all.'

Without saying it aloud, I think, 'I wonder how he managed to get to sleep without jerking off? I could never have done it.'

As always, it's as good as ever: the pleasure's different each time, each time stronger. Our bodies move in perfect unison. I put my mouth to Laura's ear and murmur, 'Christ, I want you to come now.' I say it two or three times and she starts screaming. At the last moment, I pull my cock out of her, put my hand where my prick was, and come all over her breasts.

The last day Laura spent at Marianne's, I came to see Sammy about eight in the evening. Laura was packing her things in a bag. She was leaving, her mother had agreed to take her back. We passed each other; heavy silences, averted eyes.

I slept with Sammy, but we didn't make love. He

82

claimed to be tired; I sensed he missed Laura's body. At dawn, the sound of a key in the lock woke me up: it was Marianne. She looked at me as if I were a meteorite that had landed in her bed. She had just returned from Poland by truck. She had gone to report on the armed Solidarity factions and was back a day ahead of schedule. She had a shower, got under the sheets. Sammy took her in his arms and made love to her. My eyes were open to the pale ceiling.

At seven-thirty, the alarm went off; Sammy got up and got dressed. I moved toward Marianne, stroking her breasts. Her mouth slid down my belly and she sucked me off. We went back to sleep.

*   *   *

I didn't see the autumn pass. Now it's winter, heavy and wet, but biting all the same: scrapings of lead in a river of mud. I'm not working. I'm spending everything I have left on cocaine. The blotch on my left arm has grown somewhat; its purple color has deepened. The cold has sterilized the odors of the night; there are fewer bodies in the city's subways and the ones that remain are bundled in warm clothes. At regular intervals, a needle digs into the vein inside my elbow, drawing my soiled blood for analysis. It's pointless, since we know nothing about the illness. We think we know more and more, when actually we know less and less.

I'm made up of pieces of myself that have been scattered about, then stuck back together anyhow, because after all, you need some sort of body. I'm just a mass of terrorized cells.

83

A bed, another bed, a purple vinyl armchair with an armrest on which I lay my left arm for the nurse to jab, luxurious apartments, maids' rooms, rough walls against which I lean my ruined body: places for love and places for sex get mixed up, but I don't find rest anywhere for more than a few stolen moments.

I still go back to where the bodies are furtive shadows, where bodies and looks meet as they tirelessly work towards their own downfall. When I leave, with the skeleton of a night with the savages behind me, the bony shell of the miracle, my back is streaked with red welts, my chest bruised by combat-boot soles, my tits burning, my pants soaked, dried spit on my face and streaks of cold piss tickling my thighs.

The savages take on the colors of the Fauve painters of the past. Somber, evanescent pastels in the jackets brushing pillars; the washed-out grays of faces; blue fragments of jeans enveloping asses, cocks and balls. The dust, the wet stains, a tear beneath the lip, none are more colored than the dark blue of the night, the smooth black of the river, or the diffused orange of the sodium lights on the far bank.

The black and white memory of the tangled bodies bears Fauve traces: Sammy and his fellows' golden color, which the darkness can't extinguish.

The TV is on, with the sound turned off. A record is spinning on the turntable: the Clash are singing 'Guns of Brixton'. The city is ripe for fire and destruction, but I remain motionless. A helmeted cop in riot gear yells, 'Fuck off, there's nothing to see!' Except the bloody face of Malek El-Esskine, who was killed yesterday. I don't understand what the newspapers mean when they write about the 'moral generation'. All I see is a tormented generation that rebels when individual freedoms are threatened. The telephone rings; it's Laura. 'Shall we get together tonight?'

'I don't know.'

To all of Laura's questions, I answer, 'I don't know,' with a world-weariness that exasperates her. I can't help it, I say anything at all. I say, 'Forget about me.'

'You don't mean that, do you?'

'No, I don't mean it . . . But I don't feel like doing anything, and I don't feel like seeing you.'

'You're wrong.'

'Why am I wrong? You have an urgent need for a stiff cock?'

'Among other things. Don't you feel like getting your rocks off?'

'I'm dying, Laura.'

'Nothing's going to happen to you. I know nothing's going to happen to you.'

I hung up. I couldn't move, I couldn't go out or jerk off. 'Nothing's going to happen to you.' Laura had said that with such certainty. An eighteen-year-old kid who doesn't know anything. For a moment, I see her altered, see her delicate beauty turn to ugliness. A witch's face: the blue circles under her eyes deeper, her golden eyes staring, oily hair pinned up in a bun, cheeks hollow and pale. To see a witch in a woman is to reject femininity.

I step out into the hall to dump a bag of garbage in the chute, and see my next-door neighbor waiting for the elevator. It comes and the doors open as I'm walking behind her. She lets out a little yelp. 'Oh hell, I forgot my shoes!' She turns to me and coos, 'Would you be an angel and hold the door? I'll be back in a sec!' I watch her as she runs back to her apartment. She's a tall, very beautiful mulatto with legs that go up to heaven. Leaning against the door of the elevator to keep it from closing, I wonder why this girl should be living with a bearded, balding guy who works for the post office, who practices the violin whenever he has a free moment yet can't get anything but false notes from the unfortunate instrument. My neighbor closes the door to her apartment and runs towards me, carrying a pair of silver shoes.

'I've got a show I'm going to!' she says.

'Where?'

'In Juvisy.'

'What are you going to see in Juvisy?'

'I'm not seeing anything, I work there. I'm a dancer in a revue!'

She brushes against me as she steps into the elevator. As the door closes, she shouts, 'I'll have to invite you one of these days!'

I dump my bag of garbage. Looking at the black opening of the chute, I think, 'If I were as slim as her, I could jump down there. It would be a good way to end it all.'

I'm lying down, unable to sleep, when the doorbell rings. I get up, pull on pants, and open the door. It's Sammy, looking as white as a sheet. 'Can I come in? Are you alone?'

'Of course, come on in.'

He sits on the edge of the bed, gets up, pulls off his jacket, goes into the kitchen to drink a glass of water. I've never seen him like this.

'What's the matter? Are you sick?'

'It's nothing.'

He locks himself in the bathroom and I hear him vomiting into the toilet. He comes out, goes to wash out his mouth in the sink. I've gone back to bed, and he lies down next to me. I rub his neck, but he says, 'I don't feel like it.'

I nearly say, 'Christ, this isn't a hospital!' but I shut up and take my hand away. Instead, I say, 'You don't feel like what?'

'Don't feel like fucking after the night I've just been through.'

'Can't I touch you without it meaning that I'm in the mood to fuck?'

Sammy rolls over on to his stomach and starts to cry into the pillow. I gently take him in my arms; he doesn't resist. 'What happened?' I ask. 'Did you have too much to drink? What's making you sick?'

'I'm not sick, it's me that's making me puke. You understand? I disgust myself so much, it makes me throw up.'

Sammy tells me what happened. He was at rugby practice; in the locker room after showers, the cop-coaches suggested to the players that they go to André's place. Sammy said yes. He climbed into the unmarked Renault, and they drove to the 16th arrondissement. They parked on avenue Georges-Mandel and got out. They buzzed an intercom, and a woman's voice said, 'Good evening. Can I help you?' The driver said, 'We're the rugby guys.'

'Please come in. Do you know the floor?'

'Yes, thanks.'

A woman of about fifty opened the door, and they followed her into a large apartment with hardly any furniture. There were about twenty naked girls there, in

87

every imaginable position. The guys there were naked as well, and older – tall and muscular. They were fucking the girls, solo or in groups, going from one to another, getting blow jobs, or just walking around, their huge cocks swinging.

The coaches and the players who had been there before started getting undressed, but Sammy couldn't make a move. 'What are you waiting for?' asked the driver. 'Drop 'em!'

There were six of them: two coaches and four players. Sammy was the smallest, and felt a little embarrassed. He's very muscular and runs fast, but the others were at least twice his size. The second coach had already joined the fray when one of the players asked, 'Can we go ahead?'

'Wait. First we'll take care of the usual.'

For Sammy's benefit, the cop explained: 'Monsieur André supplies the girls, and you'll be able to do anything you like with them, but first, you have to do him a little favor. Follow me, you guys.'

They walked down a dark hallway and the cop knocked at a locked door. 'Yes?' The cop and the four players went into the room and closed the door. A well-built man of about forty was standing in the center of the room, with irons around his ankles, his arms held in a V over his head by chains hanging from the ceiling. His very blond, almost white hair was cut very short; his body was hairless, his crotch and legs shaved. A young guy wearing a black nylon jacket, army-surplus pants and combat boots was whipping the chained man with a leather belt. He stopped when he saw the others come in. 'Ah, the rugby players,' the man said. 'That's what I like!' The young guy stepped back a few steps. The cop said, 'Monsieur André, there's a new one, Sammy; you know the others.'

A man was sitting in a corner of the room, near a table

piled with whips, ropes, leather harnesses, nipple clips, stainless steel rings, candles, hoods and leather pants. Monsieur André spoke to him: 'Pierre, go and play for a while and come back later.' The man got up and left, taking the young guy in fatigue pants with him. 'Let's go,' said André. 'I'm ready.' The cop pushed one of the players forward: 'Go on, Thierry.'

Monsieur André closed his eyes. Thierry went behind him and spanked him a bit; then he clenched his fists and went from spanking to punching: on his ass, his back, his kidneys. Sammy averted his eyes and tried to leave, but the cop held him back. 'Stay here and watch.' Sammy saw that the cop was starting to get a hard-on. Thierry walked around to face the chained man, kneed him in the balls, slapped his face a few times, butted him in the stomach, punched him full in the chest. Monsieur André still had his eyes closed, a smile on his lips. He was hanging like a corpse from the chains attached to his wrists.

Abruptly, he opened his eyes, looked at Sammy, and said, 'I want to try the new boy.' The cop said, 'Sammy, get your things.'

Sammy came back with his clothes and his sports bag. Monsieur André motioned him closer, and said softly, 'Put on your shorts and your jersey, and your studded boots.'

Sammy got dressed. 'Come here,' said André. 'You can do whatever you like with me, anything at all.' So Sammy came right up to him and spat in his face. He stood motionless for a moment, and then his violence exploded in a drunken bout of punches and kicks.

Pierre came back into the room. Sammy used the instruments piled on the table, then unhooked the chains and made Monsieur André lie down at full length. He stepped on to him, and walked all over his body with his studded boots. Monsieur André was jerking off with his right hand, the chains jingling in rhythm with the up-and-down movement of his wrist. He came, and his sperm mixed with the mud from the rugby field that had fallen from the studs. Pierre looked at Sammy's shorts. Sammy had a hard-on.

'Not bad for a beginner,' said Pierre; 'You've got imagination!' Then, to the cop: 'It's unusual for it to give a guy a hard-on the first time.' The cop nodded. He said to Sammy, 'OK, now go and see the girls.' Sammy backed towards the door as if he was waking from a dream. He bumped into the wall, took his boots off, opened the door, went out into the hallway. Behind him, he could hear Pierre say, 'I hope we meet again. Do you know anything about alchemy?' Sammy crossed the room where the orgy was underway, walked to the apartment door, opened it, and found himself on the landing. He threw on his clothes and ran down the stairs. On the pavement, he staggered a few steps, looked up to the sky, saw the blackness smudged by a halo of smog. He leaned over, fell to his knees, and vomited into the gutter next to a gleaming Harley-Davidson. Not knowing where to go, he came to my place.

We're still lying side by side. 'Do you understand why I make myself sick?' Sammy asks. I don't answer; I have nothing to say. I don't even know if I'm surprised. I think of my nights. I think of Laura; how far will our violence go when we're making love? Sammy speaks again: 'Shit, I did that . . . and it gave me a hard-on! It's true, it gave me a hard-on!'

I unplug the phone, switch on the answering machine, and turn off the light. We go to sleep back to back, without touching, separated by chasms of white sheets Laura and I have stained with sex.

Next morning, Sammy gets up early to go to work. He makes himself coffee in the kitchen; I stay in bed. I don't mention what he told me about last night. He calls Marianne and they have a fight; she wanted to have him with her last night, and he didn't come home. Sammy's tone is terrible: cold and lifeless. He hangs up. 'That stupid bitch is a pain in the ass!' He kisses me, says he's leaving.

'Why don't we move in together?' I say.

'Here?'

'No, I'll find a big apartment.'

'Why not?'

After Sammy leaves, I notice a red number '1' on the answering machine's message counter. I rewind the tape and listen. 'This is Laura, it's two in the morning, and I can't sleep, answer me . . . Please answer, I know you're there. I don't care if you aren't alone, come on, answer me . . . I'm sure you're with some guy, I can even tell when you're with Sammy, I can feel it. But let me talk to you. Why are you doing this? It won't do you any good . . . *Beep*.' Laura had fallen silent, and the answering machine is designed to hang up automatically if the caller doesn't say anything.

*   *   *

I visit an apartment in the 20th arrondissement on top of the Ménilmontant hill. I like the names around there, Belleville, place des Fêtes, Crimée, Jaurès. It's completely different from where I'm living now. The building belongs to an insurance company. The apartment is big, on the second floor above a Prisunic department store. It's somewhat dingy and noisy, but for 900 square feet, the rent isn't excessive.

I call the insurance company and tell them I'll take the apartment. They'll paint the place but can't do anything about the noise: I'll have to sound proof the windows myself. I call Sammy and tell him we can move in on 1 January. 'Are there two rooms?' he asks.

'Of course! I know you aren't gay!'

*   *   *

Jaime rings up. He has to see me, he says, it's important, and he'd rather not discuss it on the phone. I can't understand why he's being so mysterious.

I meet him in the café at the corner of the rue Guy-Môquet and avenue de Saint-Ouen. I've often waited for him there, standing at the bar drinking whiskies and treading on cigarette butts, spit and the dust of the end of the day; hellish minutes when I would wipe my forehead, my cheeks and my nose, looking around for him every few seconds. At last, he'd show up with the coke. In a moment, we'd go up to his place to do a line, but he wanted a beer first, and it took forever; why couldn't he drink faster?

We would prepare two lines and snort them. Three quarters of an hour later, we'd do it again, and then more and more often, every fifteen minutes. We wouldn't stop, we felt as if we were exploding. We'd talk, listen to Chris Isaac and flamenco, classical and also Los Chungitos. We'd play 'Ay que dolor' by the Hot Pants five times in a row and I'd go wild. Surrounded by posters of Brando, Jim Morrison and James Dean, Jaime would talk about his

92

disappointments: wrecked friendships, being in jail, selling clothing at the flea market. It was like flamenco: nostalgia, fatalism, tragedy past, present and future. But never anything depressing, no bleakness, no oppression; we felt we'd live forever. To temper the effects of the cocaine we'd go back downstairs to the bar and drink gin or whiskey.

For once, Jaime is at the café ahead of me. He tells me a confused story about how I absolutely must come with him to a meeting at the Porte des Lilas. 'Start the car,' he says, 'and I'll explain.'

It's seven o'clock in the evening and the rue Championnet is jammed with traffic. I get furious. 'Calm down,' he says, 'this meeting is worth it, I promise. I'm the assistant on this commercial. I'm friends with the director, and he's looking for a young chief cameraman who understands what he wants. The clients have suggested the English, the best in the business, but he's turned them all down. You've got a chance.'

Driving up avenue Gambetta, we pass Jean-Marc's place, a screenwriter friend. 'Stop here,' Jaime says, 'and we'll go up for a minute. I've got something to give him.'

Jaime presses the bell. Jean-Marc opens the door, seems surprised to see me, tells us to come in. We follow him into the living room. Astonished, I stop and take in the scene: a buffet has been set up, and twenty or thirty people are standing around, laughing and greeting me. They're friends, and Jean-Marc has got them together to celebrate my signing a contract as chief cameraman on Louis P—'s next feature film, to be shot in Lisbon. It takes me several minutes to recover from my surprise, and I tell everybody that I'm really pleased.

Marc is there, so is his girlfriend Maria, my parents, Omar, lots of other people. Laura came with Sammy who stopped by to pick her up.

I'm talking with Louis. Once again, he can't believe I'm HIV-positive. He repeats what a lisping public relations guy had told him: 'Of course he isn't HIV-positive. He's just putting on airs, trying to be eccentric. In any case, it's impossible; he's completely asexual!' I burst out laughing.

The first time I ever worked on a shoot was with Louis. I was the second assistant cameraman, and he taught me everything without once mentioning film. I used to listen to his complaints, when he'd rage like a crazy old painter, disgusted at fashion, stupidity, the crap that was turned out in the eighties, and the way French film-makers had copped out, filming nothing but empty spaces devoid of feeling. Louis grumbles in this desert, and throws his work and his wisdom in the face of conformity. He doesn't have any children and, several times, I briefly felt like the son he never had. You don't meet many people like Louis in a lifetime: I know.

The evening wears on, I go from one person to another, drink a fair amount, and snort coke in Jean-Marc's bedroom. Watching Laura, I feel she's changing before my eyes. Talking with Véronique, she turns pale. Maria watches her with hate in her eyes. Laura sees my mother joking with Sammy, comes over to me, and says, 'Your mother doesn't like me. Look at her, she's closer to Sammy than she is to me, she's pushing me away. She prefers to have you sleeping with a guy than with a girl, is that it?' I tell her to calm down, that this is a party, and no time to go looking for problems that don't exist.

Sammy is drunk. He drags me into the hall, makes me step

into the bathroom with him. We close the door and kiss, hugging each other tight. I feel his cock through his jeans. We step out of the bathroom, laughing, to find Laura standing in front of the door. She opens her mouth to scream, but controls herself, then tells me, 'You're a fucking son of a bitch!' To Sammy: 'Fuck off, you little turd! Are you happy, spreading your shit everywhere?' He walks off chuckling, muttering, 'Stuff it, you bitch.'

Laura is crying in Jean-Marc's bedroom. Véronique tries to comfort her, finally comes to get me. 'You're the only one who can help,' she says. I enter the room, see Laura in tears, and say: 'Did you really have to fuck this evening up for me?'

'Why are you being like that? Véronique told me you drove Carol crazy. Is that true? It seems she had some sort of breakdown and is paralyzed.'

'What sort of bullshit is that?' Véronique is backing towards the door, and I grab her by the arm. 'Why are you spouting this garbage?'

'Isn't that what happened?'

'It's complete bullshit! Go on, get the fuck out of here!'

Seeing me come over to her, Laura calms down a little. All I want to do is to get out of this room, and she senses it. With a defiant look, she says, 'Do you know what Maria told me? That she showed you how to treat a woman, that before you went to bed with her you didn't have the slightest idea. She cheated on Marc for that? Just to teach you how to screw a girl?'

Everybody's left except Sammy, Laura, Jaime, Marc and Maria, Sylvain and Véronique. Jean-Marc starts cleaning up. I bring the dirty glasses to the kitchen, followed by Sammy. He kisses me, I devour his lips, turn my head: Laura is watching us. She leaps backwards, yanks open the front door and races down the creaking stairs, screaming like a wounded animal. I race after her and catch up with her on the pavement. She's gasping, still screaming, not sentences, just the most urgent words: 'Why . . . You'll never love me . . . I'm all fucked up . . . You prefer that little hustler. I want to die!' She breaks away, runs to my car and kicks it, shattering a headlight. Windows open, people start yelling. Laura's still screaming. A police car stops in the middle of the intersection. They want to take her in, but Jaime intervenes, tells them she's just drunk, that it's nothing, that I'll take her home.

I shove Laura into my car, start up and roar off, leaving the others on the pavement without even saying goodnight. I'm taking her back to her mother's. She calms down. 'I'm sorry, but I couldn't stand it. You were kissing him like you've never kissed me. Couldn't you be more careful, make sure I didn't see that?'

'What about you? Couldn't you have had a little respect for this evening?'

'Because you think you treated me with respect?'

I watch Laura enter the building. She can't find her keys, leans on the intercom button, wakes her mother.

Unable to sleep, she vomits all night long: a bit of booze, the cursed party's petit fours, then bile and still more bile; the only substance filling her body's emptiness.

*   *   *

96

A production company has offered me a job as chief cameraman for a music video to be shot partly in Paris and partly in Lyon. I learn that the singer had asked that I be hired; she had seen several of my films and had liked my lighting.

We've shot sixteen hours in a row, and I'm wasted. The head of Shaman Video kept his word: Sammy has moved up from gofer to assistant. He's working with me. He takes pains, and I congratulate him. So I've done a good deed for once, I tell myself: he's a lot better off now than when he was breaking into apartments with his old friends from Stalingrad. We say good-night on the pavement, and he heads back to Marianne's.

I walk towards the gate in front of my apartment complex. The courtyard is deserted, the air biting. Shutters bang against the walls in the wind. I take the elevator, open my door. In the darkness, I can see the red number on the answering machine: eight messages. I listen to them as I get undressed. Laura's voice is on the last one. 'I gather you aren't there and must be out shooting, so I thought I'd take the opportunity to wish you a happy birthday. That's all. 'Bye . . . *Beep.*'

Her voice was cracking. I'm glad Laura hasn't forgotten me. What with the job, the apartment and Sammy, I haven't been thinking about her. I'll call her tomorrow.

Another December night. Laura lies across my bed, my head between her legs. I rip her panties with my teeth, stick my cock through the tear and slide into her. Again, that feeling that it's never been so good. But after we come, I'm still not able to take her in my arms. I imagine it

97

must hurt her. But I save that kind of hugging for boys.

After lovemaking, in the bluish light filling the studio, Laura lights a cigarette, gets up, takes a few steps. She sees the full boxes lying on the floor. 'Are you moving?' I sense a trap, but can't see why I should lie. My voice isn't very steady as I say, 'I've found another apartment, a much bigger one.'

'Where?'

'In the 20th arrondissement.'

'That's a long way away.'

'I'm not renting it alone, you know. I needed someone to split the rent.'

'So you thought of Sammy!'

'How did you know?'

'I don't know, I just suspected.'

Laura's eyes glitter with a mix of fury and terror. 'He got what he wanted,' she says. 'Sammy's pretty strong; he's stronger than me.'

'What do you mean, "got what he wanted"? I'm the one who suggested he live with me.'

'Is that a fact?'

It's one of the last days of December; the cold is biting, the sky gray and yellow. It's going to snow. I'm at a camera rental company in Vanves, checking out the equipment I'm to take to Lyon tomorrow for the shoot.

I've eaten dinner alone. I open the door to my studio. Before anything else, before I even turn on the lights, I look at the number of messages on the answering machine. It's become an obsession; I'm caught by the red number on the counter. I'm waiting for voices, signs of the outside world, Laura's words, a fixed point, a buoy I can cling to, to keep my head above water, to swim in a sea of terror.

Fourteen messages. I fast-forward through them until I hear the voice I'm waiting for:

'Hello, it's me, Laura . . . *Beep*.'

'. . . *Beep*.'

'Yeah, it's me again, I get the feeling you're there . . . *Beep*.'

'. . . *Beep*.'

'You really don't give a damn when I say I miss you. I'm not going to pester you, I know you have to get up early to go to Lyon, so please answer if you're at home. Maybe I'm mistaken, and you really aren't there . . . *Beep*.'

'I'm really sorry to call so often, but since I can't talk to you, I talk to your answering machine. It's more faithful than you; it didn't decide to go and live with Sammy. You know how lucky you are? Here you've got a little girl who's at her place and who thinks about you all the time, and you don't give a damn. Lots of guys would like to be in your place . . . Of course it's true that you prefer little boys, but you have to do what you can with what you've got! This could go on for hours . . . I'm talking to your machine so I don't have to talk to myself. Next time, I'll just tape myself and send you the cassette, it would be simpler . . . What am I doing at this moment? I'm reading Nabokov's *Tyrants Destroyed*. It's very good. Besides that - what? Not much, actually. I'm about to pack my bags to go and visit my grandparents in Cannes. What else am I doing? Fuck all. I'm not doing anything else . . . *Beep*.'

'What else am I doing? I'm smoking a lot. I smoke to forget . . . that you drink! No, not that you drink, but that you aren't there. It's becoming an obsession, there isn't even any desire, that's hard . . . You call and call, you wind up just calling from force of habit. So I wait and wait, and you aren't there. And even if you were there, what difference would it make? I'm so afraid . . . I'm afraid . . . I'm afraid of everything . . . I'm afraid of evil . . . *Beep.*'

I'm lying on the bed in my underpants. The phone rings, but I don't answer. Paralyzed, I listen to Laura's voice on the answering machine, but it doesn't occur to me to pick up the receiver. I slowly rise and turn the volume up. Just then, Laura is saying, 'So you see, it's the story of someone who is always looking for love. And one day he finds it. But he's afraid of losing it. He's so afraid, he does everything he can to lose it. He waits, he waits so long, it wrecks his nerves and his health. He's waiting for love to return, only he doesn't know if it will, so he gets provocative and demanding, even offers himself. Nothing happens until one day love comes back, very strong. He's happy, because he didn't expect it. He feels happy and does everything he can to make it last, because he knows he once did everything he could to lose it, and this time he's going to keep it. Unfortunately, it doesn't work; the more he tries to keep this love, the more love disappears, which is normal. But it shouldn't be normal, you shouldn't have to pay so dearly for happiness. So he gets beaten down, he pays and pays, he suffers for it. And he pays so much . . . Oh, no! . . . He thinks he's going to lose it again, because he's given so much. Anyway, there you are; this can go on for hours. Here's another story: This one's about someone who is looking for love and once he has it, doesn't want it, because he doesn't know it's really love. He thinks he'll find love among other people, but that isn't it. Love can be anywhere, you just have to take an interest in it, really try to catch it. But you have to want it; you have to make yourself want it, but he doesn't take the trouble. He has love in his hands, but he drops it, lets it go, and he'll never find it again . . . *Beep.*'

Christmas with the family: my father, my mother and me. My father had a heart attack at the end of the summer. Tobacco, alcohol and heredity have left his arteries clogged and fragile. His own father died of a stroke after having a leg amputated. In September, they operated on my father, cutting his right thigh open from groin to knee. The doctors told him to take it easy; and no more cigarettes or alcohol. But I know he won't take their advice; he'll start smoking and drinking again, won't ever take a vacation. He's putting it out of his mind, acting as if none of this were real. I told my mother I was HIV-positive, and she told him. 'So what?' my father said. 'Nothing's going to happen to him,' with the same certainty as Laura. Is this total love? Denial? Or a frightening courage?

I look at my father and wonder which of us will die first. My mother puts a roast leg of lamb on the table, and I catch her eye. She's in the depths of despair, as if she heard the question I was asking myself. She's probably asking herself the same question, in different terms. She's exhausted. She has put aside the life she was leading to face the twin threats hanging over her son and husband. It's worse than if it had been her. And yet she has to be here, can't turn aside. She's here because someone has to say, 'What's the matter, are you dreaming? Claude, carve the lamb and help yourselves before it gets cold!'

If Christmas was a wall of silence, the New Year is loneliness. The end of December is a mistake on the calendar, a hole in space and time. And each year is worse: there's less and less joy, more and more commercialism, stomachs crammed with turkey and ice-cream logs, and the city decorated by the ministry of tinsel. Laura is at Cannes with her grandparents.

That's it, midnight has come and gone, it's a new year. Hugs, shouts, streamers and confetti, papier-mâché joy.

I'm slowly driving down the rue Sainte-Anne - it's a pilgrimage. Nobody is stirring except a few Arabs, high or sick or both, and a couple of drag queens on the prowl. At the corner of the rue des Petits-Champs, one of them smiles at me. I park the car, and he climbs in, a mulatto with long, black, curly hair, and pointed breasts under a fake fur jacket. We talk for a long time. I tell him I'm thirsty, I'll buy him a drink. He gets out, tells me to follow him. Watching him in front of me, his ass swaying in a leather miniskirt, I wonder if I'm going to fuck him. I don't mind paying, but I'm not sure I feel like having sex. What excites me is the release of our memories; nostalgia laid bare.

He walks into the Anagramme. I can't believe the place is still here! I used to go there six or seven years ago for spaghetti with tomato sauce just before dawn. It hasn't changed: the black paint on the walls, the mirrors, the faces softened by the dim lights, a mixture of heaviness and lightness, of deep pessimism and joyful energy.

I drink a Cointreau tonic that glows a ghostly white under the black lights. Mia wets his/her lips with a whiskey and Coke. She tells me about a lover who took her travelling. 'He was from Piedmont, had the biggest cock in Italy. In Tangier, he used to bang it on bar counters.'

Another transvestite enters the bar. She rushes over to our table, half laughing, half crying, and kisses Mia on both cheeks and me on the lips, saying, 'Hello, darling!' Mia asks her what's happening. She says she was in a bar when a guy – a real one, not a fag – started giving her the eye. She smiled back, and they wound up talking. The guy took her to his place, but just when she expected to be ravished, he pulled up her skirt and started to give her a blow job. 'Can you imagine,' she says, laughing and crying, 'being taken right from the start for the opposite of what you're pretending to be?'

*   *   *

January. I've hired a van to help me move; Sammy is helping me pile my things into it. A white mist rises where our breath hits the cold air. From time to time our glances meet and we smile like accomplices. Total euphoria. We drive to the far end of Paris under a blue sky awash with metallic light.

We unload my things in the new apartment. Night falls; we don't have gas, electricity or a telephone. We buy candles and a butane lamp.

At two in the morning, we ring the bell at Marianne's flat. She opens the door with sleep in her eyes, can't understand what I'm doing there. She was expecting Sammy – alone – and the warmth of his body against her in bed.

But he says, 'I've come to pick up my things. I'm moving out, we found a big apartment.' Marianne collapses on to a chair. But only for a moment. She stands up, and says, very crisply, 'Hurry up, I'm sleepy!' She's looking at me as if to say, 'Don't celebrate your victory too soon. Sammy will come back to me. His crush on you will pass, and the sooner the better!'

Playing that game was the last thing I wanted, and I've

never considered Marianne a rival. But it's true that I feel I've won a battle; I can't help it.

*   *   *

I left a few things and my answering machine in my studio in the 15th arrondissement. Laura is still in Cannes. The phone rings; it's her. She doesn't know I've moved. Why don't I ever call her? she asks. The minutes pass: ten, fifteen, twenty. We don't say anything. She just repeats, over and over again, 'I have things to tell you.' I can't stand this conversation. 'Laura,' I say, 'I have a date and I've got to take a bath.' We go on talking, my mind is elsewhere. My nerves are on edge and I feel a blind rage rising in me. I start to scream insults at her. She defends herself, yelling, 'You've got that guy on the brain, and that's all you can think of. Does he fuck you, at least? I'm sure he doesn't. You must stand in front of him with your tongue hanging out like a dog, making cow eyes and hoping he'll be good enough to fuck you once every two weeks. Christ, it's pathetic!' I scream, 'You're a pain in the ass, you stupid fucking cow!' and hang up.

The phone immediately rings again. 'Yes?' I say. I hear Laura's voice and hang up. It rings again. I pick up the receiver and yell, 'What the fuck do you want, you stupid bitch?' and hang up. I switch on the answering machine and run the bath water. The phone rings twice, and the answering machine clicks on. I can't resist turning the volume up. I hear Laura, her voice distorted by the machine, but it's her just the same, floating in the room,

104

spying on my every move, trying to guess my thoughts before I have them.

'Thanks again for doing this to me,' she says. 'And you had to do it when I was far away. Yesterday, I was having something to eat down by the beach. I was looking at the sea, just remembering this summer . . . And I felt like calling because I was thinking of you. And then I thought, It's really over. I don't know why, because of you, because of me, who knows? I told myself I just can't go on, I'm sick of loving someone who doesn't love me. Or if he loves me even a little, he doesn't show it. So there you have it. I wanted to tell you that, but you don't give a damn, because you don't believe it. I'd rather not believe it either, I swear, it gives me the shivers. I'm cold . . . *Beep.*'

Another ring; the voice on the answering machine: 'It's me again. You don't have to answer. In fact, it might be better if you didn't. You'll just get angry again because you don't feel like saying anything nice to me, so stay in your bath. It's really a waste of love, waste of sex, waste of everything. Listen, I think I'm going to keep my memories, and try to change . . . erection! . . . change direction! And I'm going to go back to my old ways, meeting guys left and right. It'll be simpler, I won't have to think about a thing, I won't expect anything of anybody. Because when you think someone can give you lots of things, you wait. And if the guy doesn't give you anything, anything at all, you feel it's because you don't deserve it. So you get nasty, you start wondering why. That's always the way it is, instead of going in the right direction, you keep going backwards, and then you fall. Well, I'm slowly getting back on my feet. I'm not all the way up yet, but when I am, and it'll be soon, in a week or a month, then I'll forget about you. I'll be able to do things, and I won't have the guilt trips you lay on me, the feeling

105

that I'm always in the way, because I'll be alone with myself. Of course, I'm already alone, and the only person I feel good with is you, so when I feel like being alone, I think of you. I have lots to learn, lots to see, but I can't get the balance I need to live normally. I'm off-center, always on the lookout for something else. It's actually a good thing, because that's what saves me. But don't bother trying to figure out what's going on with me . . . *Beep.*'

A few seconds of silence, then the ring of the telephone and again, Laura's tinny voice from the speaker. 'This is my last message. I'm not going to bother you anymore, because I just get on your nerves. I hope you're enjoying your bath. I hope you have a nice evening, I hope you have fun, have a good time with lots of people and then you won't ever think of me again because you shouldn't. I don't know how you love me, but honestly, I don't know what love you have to give. I've had very good times with you, and others that made me miserable. Now life is going to be dull and empty. But I can't go on living this way because it feels as if I have to pay too much for the moments of happiness with you. Anyway, you don't want me any more, and I'm too aware of it, and it makes me bitchy.' I pick up the phone and try to talk, but nothing comes out. Laura heard the receiver being picked up, and I hear the hope in her voice: 'Hello? . . . Hello? . . . *Beep.*'

Another ring, her voice: 'Be sweet, this is my last message, answer me. I don't want to cry myself to sleep. If I start crying, you'll have won . . . I'm all choked up. It's hard to leave you, you've got to help me . . . *Beep.*'

'Listen, you're right not to pick up the phone, it makes me feel . . . Actually, it doesn't make me feel anything . . . *Beep.*'

'. . . *Beep.*'

'Death, death, death, death . . . *Beep.*'

'Do you remember the day when I was lying on my bed crying and I said you'd never love me? "You'll never love me! You'll never love me!" I don't think I was wrong, because if I had been, we wouldn't be where we are. I've done everything I could for you, and yet you actually love me less than I love you . . . I don't even know where you stand. But you'll regret what you've done. I want to hear your voice so much, I'm going to call often. If only to forget about you . . . Well, that's stupid. You see what you do to me? That's it. I can't get a grip on myself because of your indifference. You don't want to take an interest in me, or do things with me. The only thing you feel like doing is fucking me, and even then it's only when you're in the mood, and I have to wait for that, and I'm not going to spend my life waiting. Me, I want you every day. But you spend so much time in your little head, you always want to do the opposite of whatever you're thinking, it just doesn't work. And you'll always be unhappy because I suppose I'm not the only one, you must play this game with boys as well as girls, it isn't normal. I'm not quite normal myself, because I don't know how to control myself or keep myself in check. When you really want something, I think you get it . . . Everything's fucked up because you'll never change, and I won't ever change either . . . *Beep.*'

'I'd like you to help me leave you, not to see you any more, or want you, or think about you . . . It's awful to be thinking about someone wherever you go. I'll never be able to go back to Corsica. It's totally pathetic to get to the point where just seeing the sea makes me think of you . . . And yet I've always hated being . . . what? Romantic. I hate that word . . . *Beep.*'

The phone rings, the answering maching clicks on, but

at first I don't hear any words, just sobs: horrible, racking sobs. 'You have no idea . . . You make me really pathetic . . . Congratulations, you've won . . . Yes, you've won because I'm crying . . . Why don't you respect someone who wants to love you, to give you everything she can? You have no idea what I'm going through . . . I'm like an animal on the phone . . . That's all I have left . . . That's all I have left . . . Speak to me, one last time, I beg you . . . *Beep*.'

'Why didn't you try to go on loving me the way you used to? Why did you stop? Why did you do this to me? It's true, you spread unhappiness, just like I said. You ought to disappear . . . Talk to me, good God, talk to me . . . Come on, talk to me . . . I'm begging you, talk to me . . . Please pick up the phone . . . *Beep*.'

*   *   *

It's snowing. The flakes melt as soon as they hit the gray asphalt, then begin to stick on the pavement curbs and along the gutters, turning into a muddy soup. By the end of the day, everything is white, and a layer of snow is muffling the noises. A dulled night.

Sammy returns from his job, burnt out; it's hard to spend an hour on the métro in the morning, then another at night to come home. When he lived with Marianne, he was right next to the place where he worked. He watches the falling snow, opens a window and leans out. Eyes shining, he talks about mountain climbing. I'm getting attached to him, though I know it's a mistake. Sammy still hasn't bought a bed; his room is empty. We sleep together and I'm getting used to spending night after night with his body close to mine, within reach of my hand.

Habit is what we will have to wrestle with, I know. Sammy is twenty, he wants everything and nothing. But I'm no more clear-sighted than he is. Contrary to what people say, we're realistic at twenty; with age, you shape experience, soften and filter it. I used to like that surgical, pornographic realism. But I'm not twenty any more, and that lost clarity won't come back to me. At times, when Sammy and I are eating dinner at the round black table, I tell myself that time could stop right then, that I couldn't wish for anything other than having his soft skin next to me later that night. Everything is backwards: Sammy is my security, and Laura is danger. But Sammy expects nothing from me but the unexpected, madness, movement; his security is Marianne.

The intercom buzzes sharply: it's Laura's mother. I buzz the downstairs door open. She steps out of the elevator, agitatedly says, 'Isn't she with you?' She comes in, sees Sammy, and is surely thinking, 'Shit, a pair of faggots! It's enough to make you puke.' I see the contempt in her eyes. Laura called her, asked her to come and get her; she was somewhere in the 20th arrondissement, she'd got lost. She was crying on the phone, said she wanted to kill herself.

Laura's mother tells me she's driven over with a 'friend' who is waiting for her downstairs. She asks me to help her find Laura.

'The 20th is pretty big,' I say.

'She said she was in a café near the métro.'

It's still snowing; the street is white. The guy is driving a Renault 5 turbo. We climb in and very slowly cruise as far as place Gambetta. I get out of the car and make the rounds of the cafés on the square, but Laura is nowhere to be found. We can't search every bar in the neighborhood, I say. They drive off, and I walk back up the avenue, with the cold and the snowflakes hitting my face. I feel strong; or rather I'm aware of the strength I once had. My bruised body was made for some other life. I dream of hand-to-hand combat, sweat and dust, swords and the crackling of machine guns. And the reality? A parade of passing bodies, AIDS, the cold, a lethargy that keeps me indoors, the muffled sound of my boots on the snow-covered pavement.

Next morning, I go down to the street and call Laura's mother from a phone booth. She'd found out that Laura is at Marc's. I call him. 'Laura slept at my place,' he says. 'She called me up last night; she'd got lost near your place. I left her my keys because I had to go out. Want to talk to her?'

After a fairly long silence, I hear Laura's voice, slow and husky. Last night, she called the studio where I used to live, and got my answering machine. She left her mother's and went to the studio. She suspected I had moved out and that the apartment was probably empty, without any furniture, or even a bed, but she wanted to sleep there. She rang and rang, rapped on the door. Nobody in. The neighbors came out into the hallway when she tried to break down the door. 'He doesn't live there any more. He moved out the day after the New Year.' She wandered through the streets of the city, crossed the snow-covered heliport. She went into the Sofitel and asked for a room. They refused, saying she had to pay in advance. Crying uncontrollably, she staggered as far as Balard, took the métro and got off somewhere in the 20th; she can't even remember which stop. In any case, she didn't know my address. She got lost, called her mother, then Marc. She took the métro again and slept at his place.

'I love you,' she says. 'I want to see you.'

'Are you free tonight?'

'You know very well I'm free; I'm always free.'

'Drop the submissive bit, will you?'

Laura is waiting for me in front of the apartment complex where her mother lives. Rue Blomet doesn't look the way it did before the summer. I'm seeing it differently, but we're the ones who have changed; we're more serious, more depressed.

The pleasure to come erases everything; we behave as if nothing had happened, as if we hadn't said a word. But away from the shadows, our eyes no longer meet as easily as they once did.

We walk into the Sofitel and I ask for a room as high up as possible. Laura gets her revenge on the hotel employees; as we're walking towards the elevator, she looks like a girl who is cutting school.

Looking at the bed, I think to myself that a whole world I've rejected has slept here: engineers, manufacturers, businessmen, salesmen and diplomats, steeped in a stink of Beaujolais and cold cuts, stolid ideas and deadly certainties.

I order up some dinner. The room-service boy knocks on the door; I open up, wearing only my underpants, but he doesn't look at me. As he rolls the table in, he's squinting at Laura, lying bare-chested on her stomach, the sheet up to her lower back, her long hair in a tangle, her face turned towards him. Walking towards the door to leave, he turns back to look at her again. I smile: who hasn't dreamed of taking a schoolgirl to a fancy hotel to make love to her?

We shout out our orgasms. Afterwards, we go down to the hotel lobby, then step into the outside elevator, a plexiglass bubble that climbs up the face of the building. As we rise above the beltway, it looks like a hernia truss cinched around a city ready to explode.

In the panoramic bar we drink blue cocktails and listen to an orchestra play out-of-date jazz.

* * *

Sandrine, Jean-Marc's ex-wife, has been handling publicity for a small theater near the rue Saint-Denis. She rings me up and inexplicably invites me to a performance of Georges Bataille's *Le Mort*. Marie alone; the corpse, whom you can't see, tells the story: the inn, the landlady, Pierrot, the dwarf, the drunkard, the wine, the vomit, the shit, the cum. I'd like to see real urine flowing, but it's nothing but words.

After the play, I cross the street with Sandrine and we go to the Doña Flor. We order coconut milkshakes, vino verde and feijoada stew.

We're a bit drunk, and Sandrine tells me about the time when she was living with Jean-Marc. They used to go to the Carousel and the Elle et Lui a lot. She knew a transvestite who called herself Lola Chanel. One evening, she bet Jean-Marc that she could do a striptease, and asked Lola to find a night club where she could give it a try. She did it wearing a dress that wasn't really made for stripping; the sleeves were much too tight, and besides, she was practically naked underneath. But she managed it, and the audience clapped like mad. Afterwards, they drank some more, and then some more. Sandrine started flirting with Lola Chanel, and wound up taking off with her, ditching Jean-Marc in the night club. She made love with Lola, who played the role of a lesbian, feeling even more female than if she'd been with a guy. Lola was living with her mother, and at eight in the morning, Lola and Sandrine were in the kitchen eating spaghetti when Lola's mother came in to fix herself some coffee. She called Lola by her boy's name, Alfredo, or something like that. Sandrine laughed like a loon.

A few months later, Sandrine wanted to buy some curtains, but didn't have any money. She mentioned this to Lola Chanel at dinner, who said it would be easy to get her 500 francs if she'd turn a trick with a john. Lola was sure he would like her, and Sandrine wouldn't have to do a thing, just watch Lola getting fucked by the guy. Sandrine refused; once she started, where would she stop?

We leave the Doña Flor and I drop Sandrine off at her place in Montmartre, on the rue Tourlaque. She's living alone, but there's a guy in her life, a writer; she plans to live with him in the Marais neighborhood. She strokes my neck, I kiss her and caress her breasts. She says, 'See you soon,' and gets out.

I'm driving along the outer boulevards. The streets are still covered with snow. At Porte d'Aubervilliers, I turn right into the rue de Crimée, then head up the rue de l'Ourcq.

Driving across the bridge over the canal, I look at the black water against the white banks. As I come off the bridge, an old Volkswagen beetle comes roaring out of the rue de Thionville on my left. I jam on the brakes, but the wheels lock on the snowy pavement. The front of my car crashes into the rear of the bug, which spins off, coming to rest against the curb.

Nobody's hurt, but the two cars can't be driven. We fill out a report. I walk home, splashing through the muddy snow.

The apartment is empty, too big for just me. Sammy isn't at home; he must be sleeping at Marianne's; they've been seeing each other again, making love again.

On the answering machine counter, a red number 35 is glowing. Since six p.m., Laura has called 35 times. She had wanted to see me this evening; I told her I wasn't free, but she'd insisted. Minutes passed, and she'd refused to hang up. She wouldn't accept that her need to see me wasn't going to be satisfied. I'd got angry and hung up. I knew she'd call back and keep on calling. I had switched on the answering machine and gone out.

I'm listening to snatches of Laura's recorded voice shrieking as I fast-forward the tape.

I'm waiting. For anything. For Sammy to come back, for another call from Laura. Nothing happens. It's the hour of death.

Laura's messages get mixed up in my sleep. Rings, dial tones, our insults and words of love heating the copper phone wires red-hot. In my dream, the burning wires sear my flesh as Laura ties me up, draws and quarters me, garottes my cock and balls.

114

The ring of the phone awakens me. I feel as though I weigh a ton; the thought of having to put my foot on the floor so terrifies me, my stomach's in knots. At every ring, a burst of adrenalin rushes through me. In a sticky panic, I walk over to the phone.

'Yes?'

'Were you asleep?'

'I got to bed late. I smashed up my car and had to walk home.'

'Did you have an accident?'

'Yeah, a guy came in from my left at an intersection, and with the snow, I couldn't stop.'

'So your car's wrecked, but you're OK?'

'Yeah, I'm fine.'

'I suspected as much.'

'What?'

'I mean, last night, after you said we couldn't get together, I called I don't know how many times.'

'Thirty-five . . .'

'Could be. I couldn't stop thinking about you. And I knew something was going to happen to you but that you were not in danger.'

'Oh, shit! You aren't going to start getting on my ass at nine in the morning with that bullshit, are you? Is this something new? What are you, clairvoyant? Fuck off!'

I hang up, walk into the kitchen to make tea. The calcium deposits in the kettle peel off in sheets and float in the water I'm heating. Sammy didn't come home at all last night; I imagine him, his head, mouth and tongue between Marianne's thighs. The phone rings; it's Laura again. But her tone has changed; this is no girl talking; her voice is husky and authoritative. I think of her hands, the hands of a grown woman.

115

'You should be careful with what you say and do,' she says. 'There are areas you don't know anything about, and you're completely useless, so don't put on any airs. Yes, I suspected that something would happen to you. In fact, I not only suspected it, but did everything I could to make it happen . . . Something not too serious, something physical; it's a warning. You should also know that ever since you told me you were HIV-positive, I've been doing everything I can to keep anything from happening to you. And for the time being the sickness isn't getting any worse, as far as I know. I'm doing everything I can, but I can also stop doing everything I can, so please, show me a little respect, and stop treating me like a piece of shit who takes second place to all the little honey-pies you feel like having.'

This time, she's the one who hangs up. Her words, like self-evident truths, came out all in a rush, and I'm thunderstruck. My unanswered questions clump into a new fear, damp and cold, chilling me to the bone. I call Laura back, tell her not to be like that. I want to know more, but she remains silent. 'What do you mean, you're doing everything you can so that nothing happens to me?' She refuses to answer. We could get together, I say. Savoring her triumph, she says, 'All right, when?'

'How about this evening?'

'If you like.'

'You want to come over?'

'You still have just the one bed, I suppose. Will Sammy sleep on the floor?'

'He may not be here; he's seeing Marianne again. In any case, he can sleep on the sofabed.'

'I don't feel like coming to your place. I don't like that apartment; it makes me uncomfortable.'

'I'll pick you up at eight-thirty. Is that all right?'

Laura has moved into my old apartment, and walking in there feels like walking into my own place. The walls and floor have my mark on them: dust; blood; words; gestures endlessly repeated in the hope of creating rituals; images of bodies – mine and others' – trapped in the bathroom mirror; piss and shit dumped into the toilet bowl at regular hours.

I'm inside her, idealized by the love she bears me, and around her, like the four walls of the studio, made ugly by all the weaknesses and vices of a past from which she was absent. Laura sandwiched between me and me.

But tonight, like every time we've made love, my erect penis and her penetrated vagina unite the two parts of myself that are piercing Laura's belly in search of her soul, in the depths of her body.

*   *   *

The sun is shining on the paving stones of the piazza di Santa Maria Novella. I'm in Florence to meet Omar; his film is being shown in a festival of young European film-makers. He arranged for me to be invited, saying I had written as much of the film as he had. Pigeons brush by, their beating wings flattening the grass around the fountain. The Minerva Hotel's shutters are closed. A blue electric bus stands out against the milky glare. A little Vietnamese girl runs through the sea of birds parked on the lawn. Her father, sitting on a stone bench, gets up and walks towards the child and takes her in his arms. He is ageless, looks like an adolescent. On his smooth face, a wisp of mustache shadows his upper lip, like a child's.

117

Laura had wanted to come with me. I pretended not to notice. In the train, I dreamed of a lover's trip – it would all be so simple. But I forget my own thoughts; they don't belong to me.

In another square, a short man with a mustache is trying to take a picture of his baby in its stroller. He walks back and forth between the stroller and the spot where he wants to take the picture. He sits the baby up on its seat, talks to it, makes faces, trying to make it laugh, raises the hood of its jacket. He's ready to take the picture but doesn't press the shutter; instead, he goes through the routine all over again, walks back to his spot, but still doesn't press the shutter. It looks like a scene in an old silent comedy. Finally, the man fetches a big inflatable cucumber, sticks it between the baby's legs, and leaves, pushing the stroller.

A few words from Omar, the lights dim, the film's first images, its final ones, the lights go up, applause.

We end the night at the Tenax, a hangar remodeled into a night club, with video screens and huge shiny metal pipes. I drink, watching the kids dancing and wetting their hair in the bathroom sinks.

I leave with Giancarlo, who looks completely drunk. In the back of the car, a girl who works for the festival organization squeezes up against me. Her name is Licia and she looks a bit like Faye Dunaway; I start to think I'm going to fuck her, and then I remember the virus. Do I tell her? Not tell her? Put on a condom without any explanation? Penetrate her but not come in her twat? It's all too complicated; I'm tired and I've had too much to drink.

The straight avenues of the suburbs, dirty buildings, a door. 'This is where I live,' says Giancarlo. There are several girls in the apartment, including one just back from New York. A guy enters and Licia cuddles up to him; he's Paola's boyfriend, a girl who isn't here. They're studying twentieth-century American literature together. The guy is writing a thesis on an American existentialist writer whose name I immediately forget. He goes to fetch *The Anatomy of Criticism*, which he calls his bible.

We slip between the cold, damp sheets of an old bed made of polished wood. Licia is still wearing her sweater and underwear, I climb on top of her, don't get an erection, stroke her breasts, and fall asleep with my head on her belly. A little later, I wake up, move away from her, and go back to sleep.

Licia gets up before I do: she has work to do at the festival. I walk into the kitchen, where Giancarlo pours me a bowl of coffee. The oilcloth, the ancient stove and the tin coffee-pot, the cracked paint on the ceiling . . . I'm in Florence, and, at the same time, in other, exactly identical kitchens: in a miner's cottage in Lille where I lived for a year; in Brussels, near the zoo, in an apartment where I crashed while I was working as assistant cameraman on a short feature.

I walk through a light rain towards the city center. On the news-stands, front-page headlines report on AIDS in Tuscany. I meet Omar back at the hotel. He plans to go to Rome to see one of his mistresses; he'll make love to her that night, and tomorrow, they'll go to Ostia to take pictures. He suggests I go with him. I refuse. I return to Paris.

Laura meets me at the railway station, holding a ball of fur in her arms.

'Who's this?' I ask.

'This is Maurice.'

'Pleased to meet you, Maurice.'

I stroke the puppy's nose and he goes into a wriggling fit. The hair on his skull is sticking straight up, punk style. He's as much a dog as an iguanadon is a dinosaur.

'What kind is he?' I ask.

'He's a lab.'

'You mean a lab animal?'

'A lab is a Pyrenean sheepdog, you idiot!'

The smell of our sex; the shouts of our orgasms; sitting at the foot of the bed, Maurice has a front-row seat in a sex-education class. He looks at us with round, black eyes.

I'm drying myself off in the orange light reflected by the bathroom walls. Laura is standing in the bath, spraying her pussy with the shower nozzle. 'Sammy dropped in while you were in Florence,' she says.

'It's unbelievable! You both say you can't stand each other, yet as soon as I leave, you get together.'

*   *   *

Brion Gysin has died.* I didn't go to the funeral; not because other people dying reminds me that I might die

---

* William S. Burroughs's co-author of *The Third Mind*, painter and writer, who used a 'cut-up' montage technique for writing. The 'dream machine' refers to this and other montage techniques for writing. (*Tr.*)

soon, but because there was someone between us: Yvan, who had introduced me to Brion but didn't want me to get too close to him. No hunting allowed; you don't get friendly with a legend in just a few hours.

Brion was Tangier, Kerouac, Burroughs, the dream machine, calligraphic paintings, *The Sheltering Sky*. A vanished world which had transformed me, and which he had survived. Yvan served the legend, but was he more sincere than me? Didn't he expect the legend to serve him? As usual, I didn't commit myself; Brion's words had given me some privileged moments.

I really loved the old gentleman, who used to drink Four Roses and smoke joints all day long. He had colon cancer, an artificial anus, and a shit-bag under his impeccable white shirt. At seventy, Brion had climbed on to the stage at the Bastille Theatre to sing rock and roll. I had filmed him doing it.

Then they replaced the shit-bag with another system that required colonic irrigation only every three days. It had changed his life. But he couldn't fuck or be fucked any more. Then came the operation: two surgeons, one in front and one behind, shaking hands in his stomach: an expensive handshake.

Nearly four years before, we'd been in a fast-food place near Beaubourg, talking about operations and hospitals. With his wonderful English accent, Brion was saying, 'I have a doctor friend who advises terminal cancer patients to get transfusions of fresh blood by the gallon; that way, you can hang on for eight or ten months. But they don't listen; they race around the world, to the United States, South Africa, Australia, Paris, London, Vienna, Zurich, Tokyo, to every cancer charlatan imaginable, who can't do a thing to help them, and they die in three months, in terrible agony.'

Hamburgers, fries, Cokes, his clear eyes on me, looking for my weak spot, trying to discern whether I was trying to climb on his bandwagon. He said: 'You know, English hospitals give you what's called a Brompton cocktail, a mixture of heroin, cocaine and morphine, with a touch of gin, so you go can off on a cloud, smooth as silk. They put it on your night-table; the patient chooses whether or not to take it. If you don't take it, they pull the plug on you! At Christmas the hospital is full of old women dying in silence, and dying, groaning men. At Easter time you wake up one fine morning and find you're the only survivor, the only one spared by the clearing-out operation from before the holidays . . . That's when Mike came into my room and said, "The name of the game is: to survive." Three months later, Mike was dying of stomach cancer.'

I feel bad that I didn't go to Brion's funeral. I'm wishy-washy, vacillating, compromised. Being with all the pseudo-artists of Parisian-ness is dulling my rage.

We went back to my place. Sammy was watching TV. Laura was pacing, Maurice had pissed on the floor. There's still only one bed, and Sammy's room is cluttered with boxes. I hand Laura a red plastic bucket and a mop so she can wipe up Maurice's piss. Suffocating, I say, 'I want a guy.' 'You can screw anyone you like,' says Laura, unfolding the living-room sofabed. 'Me, I'm sleeping here!'

Sammy is forced to choose between my bed and the living-room sofa with Laura. Naturally, he chooses Laura. They huddle together, caress each other a little. He strokes her cunt, she plays with his cock. He wants her to take off her panties, but she refuses. If Sammy thinks this is her way of saying that she doesn't want to go any further, he's wrong; Laura loves making love while still wearing her panties.

I wake up in a foul mood. Sammy and Laura are still in bed. Maurice has pissed and shit on the living-room carpet. I shake Laura, and she opens her eyes. 'If you don't mind, I'd like you to get up and clean up after your pet; at breakfast, it's a real treat.'

Sammy mumbles and climbs out of the sheets. Then he does a virtuous whore act; naked, his cock half-erect, he curves his back in a long stretch, brushes against me, and walks to my bedroom, swaying his hips. I watch his ass, and Laura catches me looking. She'd strangle every faggot on the planet if she could.

Sammy has got back in my bed. I stretch out next to him, lay my left arm on his shoulders. Laura is rinsing the mop in the sink.

The sound of the water stops. Laura pushes the door open, holding Maurice. Crying softly, she murmurs, 'It's too disgusting . . .' Her face disappears.

I find her by the front door, leafing through my address book. She throws it on the ground and pulls on her jacket. The front door slams.

I go back to my bedroom, take Sammy's body in my arms, but don't get any kind of response; he's completely motionless. I'm hugging a statue of warm flesh.

Carol calls. She tells me that Laura called her and they talked for nearly two hours; that's why Laura had been going through my address book. 'She wanted to meet me,' Carol says. 'I turned her down. Have you found a new girl to be your audience? New creatures? Other sources of inspiration? As far as I'm concerned, I don't have any more time to waste; I'm leaving fiction to you. And don't ever bother calling me; I have no desire to see you.'

I've hardly hung up when the phone rings again. It's Laura, calling to tell me that she's just talked to Carol. 'So that's already two chicks you've fucked up. You know, you make people so miserable you should get a rope and hang yourself . . . I don't plan to suffer in silence. I'm not Carol!'

*   *   *

Sammy has bought a bed and fixed up his room; he's sleeping in it. I'm staring at the ceiling; dawn has broken, and the light is slanting through the slats of the blinds. I haven't shut my eyes all night: a gram of cocaine is dissolved in my bloodstream. I'm out of tranquillizers and sleeping pills.

I stagger to the drugstore, the white sky burning my eyes. I buy some Nembutal over the counter, and wash down four tablets with a cup of coffee. The phone rings. The answering machine is on, so I don't pick up the receiver. I turn up the speaker volume: it's Laura's voice, speaking in a tone I've never heard before. I listen, paralyzed by the drug.

'I've made a decision. First, you're going to move out; second, you're breaking up with Sammy; third, you're never looking at another guy in your life; fourth, I'm leaving you; fifth, you're going to be alone, all alone. In a word, I no longer wish you well . . . *Beep*.'

124

I get undressed in the bathroom and examine every part of my body reflected in the mirror, looking for other pink blotches. I find one on the triceps of my right arm. The one on my right biceps has grown larger and turned dark purple. I lie down; the tablets begin to take hold and I fall asleep.

While I slept, Sammy went off to work and Laura called constantly. When I awoke, the red numbers on the counter indicated twelve messages. I listen to them:

'I forgot to add one thing, and that is that there's a solution for all this, but you, my dear, must be the one to find it. And you'd better, for your own sake . . . *Beep.*'

'The pity of it is, you're fucking up your life. What you don't realize is that you aren't just fucking up the moment, but everything that follows, because it's going to stay with you. You won't have me, but you won't have anyone else, either, because no one will be attracted to you. You aren't aware of all this. It's your downfall, and you will have brought it on yourself . . . *Beep.*'

'I can really be mean first thing in the morning! I hate fatalism. For us to end up here after eight months proves that you really can do shit. You're gay and you'll always be gay. You'll carry that all your life, until the day you die. At fifty, if you're still alive, you'll be an old fag. People aren't made to live that way, or if they do, things have a way of . . . happening to them. People who wreck or destroy things are punished, that's the way the world is. Punished by what? By people like me, by diseases, by all sorts of things . . . And you're in it up to your neck, you still don't get it, that's the sad part, and the less you understand the closer you get to dying. You're making matters even worse: with the message you have on your answering machine, it really sounds as if you're living shacked up with a guy . . . *Beep.*'

'I hope you're there and can take in what I'm saying. But you have to realize that things don't happen by accident. You're where you are right now because that's the way it was meant to be. It's your downfall! . . . *Beep.*'

'Everything I'm doing now is because I hate faggots; I hate them, hate, hate, hate them! . . . *Beep.*'

'If you're there, you ought to answer; it's in your own interest. You may have been pretty lucky up to now, but your luck is going to change fast, very fast – very, very, very fast! It's to be expected. And your closing up, and not standing up for yourself, isn't helping your case. Of course, maybe you're already dead . . . You see how awful it is to push someone to make them no nasty? You have a gift for it. So what are you doing? Are you fucking, at this hour? A good-looking boy! A real hunk! . . . You're gambling with your life, and you aren't going to win! . . . *Beep.*'

Laura in a high, little-girl voice: 'Hello, hello, it's me, Carol, hello. Hello, listen, I want to suck you off . . . hello . . . Ha, ha, ha! hello, hello . . . *Beep.*'

'Hello, hello, this is the game of life . . . Your fate lies in your hands, my friend . . . The choice is yours: either you win life, or you win sudden death, it's up to you. All I can say is, death is on your face, so hurry up. Hurry, hurry, hurry, because I'm very frightened by what I'm doing, very, very frightened. And don't think it's blackmail; I can see death on your face. I'll tell you all about yourself, because it's really vital . . . And I'm not indifferent to your downfall, because it causes mine . . . *Beep.*'

After a night of drugs, the phone messages are another kind of drug; words soaring over the city from one arrondissement to another, high-pitched beeps, threats. And what if Laura were right? She dares tell me things that nobody else does. My friends play up to me and reasssure me; she sees my weaknesses and spits them in my face. I've betrayed her; she believed in love, in the first love of her life, and I was just looking for salvation, a few moments of calm and security.

I'm carrying death, and it's weighing on my shoulders. I'm sinking, going down for the third time. I get on the phone and spend a long time talking to people, anyone at all. When I reach my mother, she doesn't recognize my voice. I tell her that I want to escape the apartment and my phone – especially the phone, which decides life and death, announces the ravages of the illness, the spread of the virus. I'm in a bad way, sliding downhill fast. Laura knows it, she told me, she's threatened to abandon me. What if she really did? My mother listens. 'Who's listening to me?' I ask. 'Are you listening?'

'Come and have lunch with us. It will do you good to get some air and think about something else.'

The asphalt ribbon is white; the sun has dried the salt spread on the roads to melt the snow. It hurts my eyes, so I put on a pair of Vuarnet sunglasses. As usual, I'm driving very fast; it's a race against time. In the turns, the rear wheels of my Alfa skid on the descent through the Fausses-Reposes woods. Between the tree trunks, the ground is smooth and white. Twenty years earlier, I used to play in these woods with my friend William. Once, when we were out biking, a boy approached us; he was probably eighteen or nineteen, but he seemed very grown up. He was gentle, he told us his father manufactured underwear for Petit-Bateau. He wanted to know what brand of

127

underwear we were wearing. We didn't mind telling him, did we? No, of course not, but we didn't know. So he had to look at the labels; the boy unbuttoned our flies and slid our pants and underwear down to see the brand. The ones I was wearing were from Eminence.

What was there to talk about? To pretend to be waiting for wonderful, liberating events, life's works of art? My mother was very beautiful once. At sixty-six, she's still a very attractive woman. But for whom? For what audience, what love, what external demand?

The big house is empty. Empty, the way it's always been, ever since it was built, ever since my childhood. And yet my mother is welcoming. That's it: an empty welcome, a serious gaiety.

'Whatever do you see in that girl,' my mother asks, 'to get in such a state?'

'Do you prefer me to be with a guy?'

'That's none of my business. We always let you be free!'

After all, perhaps the land of the spirit is flat, as ancient geographers portrayed it. And in the center, not Jerusalem, but Laura, her love, a virus, the hopelessly tangled threads connecting me to life; and all around, *terrae incognitae*: obscure vices, hidden suns, futile hopes.

I had left my apartment knowing that I would only be out for a few hours, that I would come back to open the door and run to the answering machine to read the number on the message counter, and to hear the voice that would decide between life and death, calm and storm: my personal meteorology.

While I was having lunch with my mother, Laura had called ten times. I sit down to listen.

128

Putting on a deep, boy's voice: 'Hello, hello, the line's been busy for an hour now! . . . *Beep.*'

Then, in her normal voice: 'Hello, answer me if you're there, because I really need to calm down. I just talked to your mother who told me you were going to have lunch with her, so you must still be here, if you aren't at her place . . . Be nice, answer me . . . Hello? . . . *Beep.*'

'Hello, answer me! I really have the feeling you're dead and I'm getting worried; it wasn't supposed to happen so soon. All right, I'm going to call your mother and tell her you're dead; maybe she'll be pleased . . . Hello? . . . Hello, hello, hello? . . . Hello, hello, hello, hello? . . . So who is having lunch with who and who isn't having lunch with who? . . Did you drag a little Chinese boy home from your take-out place in Belleville? Unless you've had your throat slit, that is. Fancy that, you with your throat cut by some faggot in the street . . . Answer me, it's for your own sake. We won't spend an hour talking on the phone, since that's what you're afraid of. Although that must not be what frightens you. Be careful, I beg you, keep an eye out. Very strange things are happening, and you aren't on the right track. You're really in a bad way . . . It kills me to think there are guys like you around, weak and worthless. But you aren't going to win. Even if you try to work, you'll turn out nothing but shit . . . In any case, I don't think you have anything left to say: you've lighted a few films, you've written a screenplay . . . There's shit left for you to do, because there isn't much to say about a bunch of faggots jerking off, if you don't mind my saying so. So are you going to answer, yes or no, because I'm getting meaner and meaner, and it hurts me for you, it makes me want to cry. I don't like being mean with you; I pity you, and there's nothing worse than pity. You're weak, and I can take advantage of you. You don't dare

129

face anything, except your work of course, and that's worthless. The less you answer, the weaker you are! . . . *Beep.*'

'The worst of it is that as long as you don't answer, I'm going to keep on calling you, so your line will be tied up all day and all night long, and tomorrow, and the day after, until I get you. So if Scorcese or Metro-Goldwyn call up with work, too bad! Listen to my first message again, things are going to turn out just the way I said they would. You'll be surprised when it happens. You're spineless, my dear friend . . . Wake up, wake up and fight. The more indifferent you are, the nastier I become, it's natural. You came to see me the night before last, and I would really have preferred you hadn't come, instead of coming and being pathetic, incapable of doing anything. You've stirred my hatred. You're fucked in any case, no matter what you do: either you kick off within six months, or you live a living hell because I'm going to make it hell for you. Or else you choose calm and peace, which means love, my dear, with a capital L, and you'll see that everything will go well with your work, your health, everything . . . *Beep.*'

Her voice breaks, moving towards tears: 'I'm begging you, answer me. You frighten me . . . Oh, I'm so frightened . . . I'm afraid, and you're not there, you don't want to be there . . . Don't leave me frightened, don't make me be mean . . . don't make me . . . *Beep.*'

She's screaming now: 'I'm going to come and set fire to that apartment of yours, and I'll burn down every other apartment you live in with Sammy . . . Shit, you really must want to die. You're a bitch! A bitch! Answer me, you god-damned fucking faggot, or all hell will break loose, I'm

130

going to wreck everything! Just you wait! You really want me to go after the people you love? You won't be the only one who's going to die. I'm going to hurt everything around you, wherever you go, your whole family is going to cop it, so I'm begging you, answer me, please answer, stop all this, it's getting horrible . . . Answer me . . . answer me . . . I'm not myself any more . . . *Beep.*'

'Have you ever heard of hellfire? . . . *Beep.*'

* * *

I'm having dinner with Sammy at the Pancho Villa, in the rue de Romainville: Mexican beer, tacos, enchiladas and mescal. The restaurant's four yards long and two wide, just a counter with stools, with red beans and brown sauce in tin pans covered with aluminum foil simmering on the electric burners. A small woman with a high-pitched voice busies herself behind the counter. She changes the tape on the cracked cassette player, and Chavela Vargas' songs carry me to towns with strange names, Oaxaca, Durango, the sun right overhead, white dust, a Colt 45 hidden under my pillow in an El Paso hotel room.

It's always the same universal song, whether it's Edith Piaf, Oum Kalsoum, tango or flamenco: the words and sounds of pain and nostalgia are born of reality, but so pure and keening they're almost holy. Suffering doesn't mean despair. The music of those songs moves people forward, fills them with the energy to live.

We go home, and everything strikes me as natural: living with Sammy, having dinner with him, going to bed, caressing each other, making love. But Sammy is twenty, and he doesn't want any rules; nothing is taken for granted. I'm the needy one, begging for a night, for a caress, for his dusky, soft skin. Night after night, I find myself caught in the very trap I wanted to avoid at all costs.

'If you want us to sleep together,' Sammy says, 'you have to come to my bed.' The phone rings: it's Laura's mother, on the edge of hysterics. 'You're the only one who can do anything,' she says. 'She's back with me, she isn't sleeping, she cries all the time, she screams, vomits, throws plates against the walls. I can't stand it any more. I have work to do, I can't spend all day keeping an eye on her. She says with just one word from you, she'd be better.'

'I have work to do too,' I say, 'and it gets on my nerves having my phone line busy all the time and finding forty messages from Laura when I come home at night.'

'Then break it off. Tell her it's over, once and for all.' I hear a muffled scream from Laura: 'No, shut up!' She tears the receiver from her mother's hands. 'No, it isn't over, tell me it isn't over.'

'I didn't say anything, your mother said that.'

I can hear her mother's voice, muffled: 'And you, why don't you just go with a normal boy who likes girls and not a fag who spends his days being fucked by Arabs!' Now I'm the one screaming: 'So that hysterical showbiz whore thinks she's "normal"? You think you're normal?'

Sammy gets up. 'The two of you can go fuck yourselves. Fuck it, I want to get some sleep!' He slams his bedroom door.

I don't want Sammy to go to sleep without me. To end

132

the conversation, I agree to have lunch with her and her mother tomorrow, and try to talk things over calmly.

Laura is waiting for me in the café on the rue Faidherbe near her film school. As I park my car, a wheel scrapes against the curb. I open my door, Laura steps out of the café, crosses the snowy street, walks towards me.

Faubourg-Saint-Antoine; Bastille; the rue de Rivoli. We're too wiped out to talk: too many words, the city, the snow, the same gestures, made over and over again.

We meet Laura's mother in a café on place du Châtelet. The discussion is pointless, full of unfinished sentences.

'You can see he's never going to change,' she says. 'Give him up.'

'Why don't you mind your own business? I love him the way he is, I just want him to try a little. You can try, can't you?'

I've stopped saying anything, and watch them have a fight. The talk gets heated. Laura curses at her mother who gets up and tosses a hundred-franc note on the table. As she leaves, she says, 'Don't come to me asking for anything to do with this guy. I have better things to do than waste my time with your nonsense!'

We order chocolate cakes, but they're nauseating. I drink two cups of coffee and get the shakes. We go out. It's a light gray afternoon; the sky presses down on our skulls like a cast iron lid. We don't know what to do any more.

*　　*　　*

Sammy has been complaining that nothing ever happens in his life. He longs for something out of the ordinary; he's thinking about his father, about break-ins. I tell him he has to choose. He's sick of spending two hours in the métro every day to go to Shaman Video in the 15th arrondissement; sick of paternalistic people who are only too happy to work him fifteen hours a day for shitty wages; sick of eating dinner across from me at the round black table, watching TV. 'A year ago,' I tell him, 'you were filing photos in boxes for two thousand francs a month!'

From time to time, he gets together with Serge, who tells him: 'What are you saving for? You've got star quality. If you really wanted to, I could make something of you.' I ask him if he still enjoys falling into traps set by faggots on the prowl. 'No, you're right,' he says, looking like a kid caught red-handed. Then it's my turn to feel sick of being the goody-goody. 'I'm not your father, dammit!'

Sammy goes out. He hangs around the rue de Lappe or the rue de la Roquette, drinks mescal at the Zorro until he can't stand up, gets into fights with skinheads, comes back with torn clothes and dried blood under his nose, vomits in the sink in the bathroom. Then he wakes me up in the middle of the night, climbs into my bed and goes to sleep, snoring. In the morning, when the alarm goes off, I have to tell him, 'Sammy get up! You're going to be late!' a dozen times, to rouse him out of bed.

It's late when I come home. Sammy is cutting coke on a mirror with a razor blade. His eyes are shining. He's been to the barber and his hair is shaved at the sides, a little longer on top. Kissing me, he says, 'Did you get yourself sucked off in a parking lot?'

'I had dinner with Bertrand.'

He makes two lines, sniffs one of them, and hands me the straw. I snort the coke.

'Me, I went back to André's,' he says. 'It wasn't bad.'

I ask for details: how many girls did he jump? Did he hit Monsieur André? He won't say. He hugs me from behind, pressing his body against my ass; I can feel his cock getting stiff. He pushes me toward the bedroom. 'I feel like fucking you,' he says. 'Strip your clothes off.'

Naked, I unbutton his army surplus pants, pull down his underwear. I get down on all fours on the bed, my back flat, arms locked, palms against the mattress, like a female dog. Standing behind me, Sammy spits in his hand and wets his cock. I spit in mine and moisten my asshole. No one's fucked me in two years; Kader was the last one, in the ruins of a devastated town.

'Put a condom on,' I say.

'I don't have any.'

'Go and get one from the bathroom.'

'No.'

'Do you know what you're doing?'

'I told you, I don't want to.' A white flash behind my closed lids. This boy is out of his mind. He loves me. Or maybe it's the risk he loves, the unknown, defying the commonplace.

Female, I shout with pleasure. I turn round, see Sammy's half-closed eyes. I grab his shoulders, his hips, pull his body deeper into me. I jerk off. We come.

*   *   *

135

I'm due to meet Laura later in the afternoon in Geneva, at the airport. She took the train; I flew, because I couldn't leave Paris in the morning. I spend an hour waiting for her on the French side; she's on the Swiss side.

She almost missed the train, she tells me. The taxi she called didn't show up, so she wandered the streets of Issy-les-Moulineaux at six in the morning with her travel bag and Maurice on his leash, hitchhiking. A guy gave her a lift to the Gare de Lyon.

We're in a bus on the way to Avoriaz, where some producers and journalists have set up a local TV station that will broadcast during the winter season. I was asked to design the lighting for the set where interviews, news and games will be shot. Jaime had been hired to run the set, and he had mentioned my name. I'm to replace a cameraman who had been fired after two days.

I'd like to get the feeling back I used to have when I first met Laura: feeling comfortable with a girl, with a woman, with an image of femininity different from the one Carol had left me with, full of groans, sadness and clumsiness. I thought we had to get away from Paris. We caress each other in the bus, but the closer we get to Avoriaz, the more distant Laura seems; she withdraws into herself, becomes transparent. We get caught in traffic jams. Night falls.

The ski lift climbs towards the resort. A horse-drawn sleigh carries us between buildings stuck in the snow like cheap spacecraft that have crash-landed there; it drops us off in front of the TV station's offices. I carry the suitcases; Laura holds Maurice; when she sets him down, he sinks up his belly in the fresh snow and rolls around.

I walk on to the set. Jaime looks a bit surprised to see

Laura. He says the director forgot to rent an apartment for me, but he can lend me his; he'll go and sleep at a girl-friend's, but hasn't decided which. Jaime has two already, and thinks he's falling in love with one of them. 'The other one's for fucking,' he says. 'She's a nice little whore.'

Formica, plastic, a green-and-white suite in a condo in the snow; Maurice shits on a newspaper in the bathroom. We eat dinner in a restaurant with Jaime; meat cooked on hot tiles.

It's a gloomy night, in spite of a snowstorm punctuated by the halos of the streetlights. But we make love, and it's good, as if in response to an unfailing pleasure principle whose source is outside of us.

Next morning, I go to work on the set. Laura meets me there around noon. We rent boots and skis. The sun is white; Didier, an electrician on the set, joins us on the slopes. We're going too fast for Laura, who stops, paralyzed, in the middle of the slope. Looking uphill, I see her, tiny and black against the light. We wait for her in a café at the bottom of the hill. In a rage, she sips a cup of hot chocolate. I go back to work on the set, she takes Maurice for a walk. I find her in the green-and-white suite.

That evening, a girl tries to pick me up at a buffet thrown by the TV station; she's a makeup artist. Laura and I don't make a gesture towards each other, and exchange only the barest of glances from time to time. The girl can't understand that we're together. She squeezes in next to me. Her sister has a Yorkshire terrier with her, and Maurice plays with it. Laura is looking daggers. 'One's even more vulgar than the other!' she whispers in my ear. Abruptly, she moves towards the makeup artist and starts to speak to her in a soft voice while stroking her arm and cheek. The frightened girl thinks Laura is a lesbian. She leaves, dragging her sister with her.

The operator tells me that Sammy called at about eight. Laura goes pale, clenching her fists until the nails dig into her palms. Walking towards the suite, she can't contain herself. 'Why did Sammy call? Can't he spend two days without calling you? Is he planning to show up here?' The snow muffles her screams.

In bed, Laura talks to me, asks questions; I don't want to answer. I don't want to make love. She jumps on me, rips my T-shirt. I'm afraid to make a move; I feel like killing her.

I finish lighting the set the next day, and the producers are amazed that it took me so little time. That evening we go to a nightclub with Jaime; half-light, mirrors, metal. I drink gin-and-tonics and we talk about this and that, just to have the feeling that we exist. Laura's body is sitting between us, but she's elsewhere.

At last we slip once more between the chilly sheets, but Laura can't sleep and starts talking again. I tell her to be quiet, but she doesn't want to let me sleep. She doesn't want to be alone, with her eyes open. She's looking at us, but it's an 'us' that is fading, slipping away.

Suddenly I completely lose control: I slap her, punch her, throw her out of the bed. She's rolling on the floor as I approach, I'm going to demolish her. She backs away, crouches next to the wall, protecting her face with her hands. Maurice pisses on the carpet.

But I can see Laura collapsing before my eyes. She's so frightened, she's losing her power over me. We're two exhausted, wounded animals. We end up falling asleep in the torn sheets.

We pack our things in the bags without speaking. At breakfast with Jaime, Laura is wearing a pair of sunglasses to hide the circles under her reddened eyes. She slaps me with all her might. 'You're crazy!' says Jaime. And Laura says, 'That's for the night you put me through!'

We take a sleigh to the taxi stand, then drive to Geneva. Two electricians who worked on the set with me are going back to Paris. I'm going to fly; Laura has her return train ticket.

We drink a glass of wine at the airport bar. When it's time to say goodbye, Laura says she wants to take the plane back with me. I can't stand the idea of her acting on a whim. 'Don't start jerking me around. Take your train and leave us the fuck in peace!' She abruptly stands up, shoving the table and knocking a glass over. She walks towards the Swissair counter, dragging a terrified Maurice by his leash. I catch up with her, grab her shoulder, pull her away from the counter. 'You have a return train ticket, and you're going to take the fucking train. In any case, you don't have money for the plane, and neither do I, and that's all there is to it!'

'Go ahead, hit me again the way you did last night. Beat me up! Get your rocks off!'

She tears away from me, drops Maurice's leash, runs toward the bar, turns around and yells, 'Haven't you done enough to me?'

Her voice echoes through the concourse. 'What more do you want?' The light-colored floor is smooth and shiny, like a glacier stretching out of sight. Heads turn to look at us. Laura screams again: 'I can't have kids because of you, I'll never be able to, isn't that enough?' Filtered by the plate-glass windows, the outside light gives Laura's face an amber glow. At the table in the bar, the two electricians try not to meet my eye. I'm white with rage and fear; she has no right to talk like that. She freezes, stops shouting: 'You're scared, aren't you? You don't give a damn about what could happen to me, but you're scared of people knowing what you've done!'

'Shut up and calm down. Are there any free seats in the plane?'

'Don't change the subject, you coward. You want to treat me like shit? The whole world's going to know what you did, I swear!'

Then Laura starts crying, sobbing and screaming. She looks around, strangled. She runs towards the exit, shouting, 'The whole world!'

I sit down. The electricians are staring into their glasses. 'It's getting worse and worse,' I say. 'Didier, can you lend me five hundred francs so I can buy her a plane ticket?' I stick the notes Didier hands me in my pocket and walk towards the exit.

Beyond the automatic doors, high fences line the path; the ground is dark red in the bright sunshine. I can't see Laura, but I find her jacket on the ground fifty yards down the path, her sweater a little farther along. I walk faster; the path turns right. There she is, beyond the turn, sitting on the ground against the fence, choking on her sobs. I kneel at her feet. Her dripping face stands out against the blue of the sky and the fence's geometric pattern. I wipe Laura's tears and gently stand her up. 'Come on,' I say, 'we'll buy you a plane ticket.' I'm holding her up, as we walk slowly, clumsily, through the no man's land between light and shadow. I speak again: 'Why do you say you can't have kids?'

'You know perfectly well why.'

'You think you're HIV-positive, but you aren't sure?'

140

'I took the test. It was positive, but I didn't want to tell you.'

I feel as if a building has crashed down on me. Words become meaningless. As if by reflex, I say, 'Shit, I can't believe it. How long have you known?'

We're back in Paris. The taxi stops; Laura gets out, I follow her, we kiss as she leans against the white body of the cab. Tenderly we say goodbye. She walks towards the gray-green buildings, I climb back into the taxi and it drives off.

We meet the next day in a café close to place de l'Alma. We apologize. I caress her a little, stroking her neck, her hands, her breasts with my fingertips. She's made up her mind to move away, stop sliding downhill. It's already too late, but she has to get away before things get even worse, before even the memory of the very good times is erased.

We turn our backs on each other: she walks towards the Alma bridge; I walk up avenue Marceau.

*   *   *

Sammy went to Toulouse and showed his father cassettes of the films he had worked on. His father borrowed his boss's Porsche and they went for a drive around town. 'That's good,' he said. 'Keep it up. I'm proud of you.'

Exhausted, I drag myself through empty days; my face pale, bluish circles under my eyes, nerves on edge, my soul

141

tarnished. Laura is eighteen years old, and her body is mortally wounded. I'm carrying a burden heavier than the threat to my own life. For the first time in my life, I've got a crime on my hands I can't wash off.

Sammy no longer sees the gleam in my eyes that he's looking for. I sense he's going to leave me. When Omar calls and suggests that Sammy and I act in a film he's going to shoot, I accept, as a way of delaying the process. Sammy accepts too, for the money, or maybe out of narcissism.

The film will be a five- or six-minute dramatization of a novel for TV. It has erotic, passionate scenes involving three characters: two boys – Sammy and me – and a girl, Karine Sarlat, a young actress we both want to sleep with as soon as we see her.

The shoot lasts three days; seduction, bodies brushing against each other, kisses, caresses, heartbreak. I'm naked on top of Karine, the camera is rolling, and I can't help getting a hard-on. But my love for Sammy comes back like a wave.

We part, promising to meet again. 'You owe me a night of love,' Karine tells me. Sammy is annoyed that he wasn't the recipient of the message. 'You're nothing but a dumb little boy toy,' I tell him.

*   *   *

With Jaime, I go to a party on the rue de Longchamp where everyone is taking Ecstasy. They sell us a pill on the way in. Some thirty people, including a few video technicians I know, a couple of actors and two popular singers, are walking around a large apartment without any furniture. Particles accelerated in a cyclotron.

But their movements gradually slow down; people touch each other; boys and girls, girls together, boys together. Nothing sexual, just touching, a need for contact. I look at Jaime and ask him if the drug is having any effect on him. 'Fuck yeah!' he says. A guy takes his clothes off, fetches some brushes and tubes of gouache, and starts painting his chest and face. Others bring ice cubes from the kitchen and rub them on their cheeks, saying 'It's beautiful! It's so beautiful!' We're right back in the seventies – except that with Ecstasy, you can't make love, because the boys can't get it up. So it's the seventies, but with AIDS and safe sex!

'You've got to come to Spain this summer,' Jaime tells me. 'I was born near Alicante, all my friends are back there, we'll have whatever we like, girls, motorcycles, we'll have a ball.' I prefer the years of the seventies with Jaime to those of this streetwise crowd on the rue Longchamp.

I still don't feel anything from the pill, and start drinking everything I can find: beer, red wine, whisky, vodka. I end up drinking straight Ricard until Jaime takes the bottle away from me. Half an hour later, I'm kneeling in front of the toilet bowl, and vomit for the rest of the night.

Jaime takes me home. Naturally, Sammy isn't there; he's sleeping at Marianne's. For the next three days, I'm sick as a dog.

*　　*　　*

143

When he found out I was going to see Karine again, Sammy came running. The three of us go out for a drive along the banks of the Marne. Evening turns to dusk: it's the hour between dog and wolf, 'when man can't tell a dog from a wolf,' says an old Hebrew proverb. I think of Laura, who said something like that the day I first met her. When we're together, we can't tell light from dark, the tame animal from the wild.

We eat in a riverside restaurant where a modern veranda has been added to the front of an old house surrounded by plane trees. We drink new red wine, laugh, talk loudly, using obscene, provocative words that cause people to look at us with disgust. But the eroticism we're feeling makes us feel all-powerful.

Karine is beautiful: long black hair, sensual lips, pointed breasts under her T-shirt. Sammy gets carried away by his talk. He wants to go join a group of alchemists in a château near Dieppe and participate in their Celtic feasts, dressed in animal skins. A member of the group bought the château; the shrine and the laboratory have been installed. The alchemists raise cattle on the land surrounding the château, and sell pottery in a small shop in a neighboring village.

Later, we leave the café and walk down the street screaming. Sammy pushes me down on to the hood of a car and kisses me full on the mouth; we roll on the ground, on the asphalt, in front of the wheels. Karine has stretched out in the back of the car, her feet against a side window; Sammy climbs on top of her. I sit down behind the wheel and take off. I drive very quickly; the lights of Paris approach and the night becomes lighter.

Back at my place, we put the mattresses from our two beds side by side in Sammy's bedroom. We get undressed

144

and stretch out, with Karine lying between us. But Sammy gets up; he goes into the bathroom, takes a razor, and starts to shave his armpits and his pubic hair. 'It's the first stage of purification,' he says, 'before beginning the Great Work.' Karine and I exchange a worried look. Sammy goes to the kitchen, comes back with a knife. He goes to stand in front of the bathroom mirror, legs spread, chest erect, and starts methodically slashing his chest, arms, and thighs with the knife. Then he takes a bottle of rubbing alcohol and pours it over the red furrows cut into his flesh. 'Try it,' Sammy says, 'it isn't fake . . . it feels so good.' Sammy has a hard-on; I feel like vomiting. I go back into the bedroom and stretch out next to Karine. We burst out laughing, 'Stop him!' she says.

'I can't bear to look.' Sammy comes and lies down too. We don't make love. Just a few caresses before falling asleep.

Next morning, I'm awakened by noises in the passage, and I suddenly remember it's the housekeeper's day. I lie motionless, pretending to be asleep. The door to Sammy's bedroom where we're sleeping is open; between my nearly closed lashes, I can see it framing the housekeeper's silhouette, wider than it is tall. Horrified, she looks at the two mattresses, the three bodies, and the blood on the sheets, then runs away as if she'd seen the devil.

Sammy and Karine are still asleep. I make myself coffee; the housekeeper has disappeared for good. I walk into the living room. There's a message on the answering machine.

'This is Laura. Just a word to say that you're following me, too. I opened the paper this morning and saw your face with that bitch Karine Sarlat! It'll at least give me the

145

satisfaction of putting the newspaper on the floor so Maurice can piss on it. So now you're an actor? Have you changed jobs because of the scenes in bed with her? Is she better than me? Does she have a job, some money? Maybe she isn't jealous. Do you fuck her really well? Did you tell her you were HIV-positive?' Karine comes into the living room, and I snap the answering machine off. I can't tell if she heard Laura's last sentence, but she's looking at me as if it's already too late for anything to happen between us.

After Karine leaves, I call Laura. She isn't there, I hear her voice on her machine: for once, I'm the one to leave a message. I tell her not to be unhappy for no reason, that nothing happened between Karine and me. I tell her I want to see her, that she can come and sleep at my place tonight.

Laura hasn't called back. I'm waiting for Sammy, who said he'd come back to have dinner with me. Edith Piaf is singing 'Les amants d'un jour' in a scratchy old documentary on TV:

> *And when I closed the door on our goodbyes,*
> *There was so much sunshine in their eyes*
> *It hurt me so, it hurt me so. . .*

Sammy hasn't come home. I watch for him from the window, but don't see him coming. I leave the apartment, take the elevator, cross the underground parking garage and get into my car; concrete and neon lights.

Other walls: those of the buildings on the place des Fêtes. On the glistening wet asphalt, I drive down the rue de Belleville. I step into the Lao-Siam. The owner says good evening; his hand feels like steel; he could crush my fingers without even trying. I imagine him as the hero of a karate film shot in Hong Kong; I think of the Jackie Chan films I used to see in a cheap Tunis suburb.

At the next table, two women are laughing like loons. I have the feeling I've seen them before. One of them tells how her car was stopped by riot police at a security checkpoint. She was with a girlfriend; they were eating fried chicken. The cop asked for the car's registration papers; the driver handed them over, covered with chicken grease. This gave her an idea for a joke to play at the next checkpoint: 'Hello, madame. Your papers, please. Are you carrying anything in the trunk?'

'Yes. Two chicks and some coke.'

The cops opened the trunk, weapons ready: inside were two fried chickens and a pack of six Coca-Colas. The two women burst out laughing.

Later, I went walking across the constantly erased footprints left by the passengers of sex. A half-moon shrouded by clouds shines on the roofs of the barges. Dust and gravel mixed. For a few hundred yards, full of an immediate desire, I am free of restraints and powers. I feel I am lord and master.

Three Harley-Davidsons are parked in front of the little Arab bar, opposite the entrance to my parking lot. I can see silhouettes leaning against the counter, leather jackets, army-surplus pants and shaved skulls. I park my car and go up to the apartment.

147

There are messages from Laura on the answering machine. I'm tired, not sure I want to hear them. Finally, I rewind the tape and run it.

'I got your message, I want to believe what you're telling me, it would be wonderful if nothing happened between you and Karine. I want to see you very much tonight, and that's a wish I don't want to have any more. And there's something else I have to tell you, and I'm not sure I dare. I don't know if I'm going to send you the letter I've written you. I would have liked to be close to you at least one more time. But I know you don't really feel like it, even if you did call this morning to ask me to come over . . . *Beep.*'

'All right, I'm calling again, and I'm talking on and on, but I think I can still afford to do it because I'd like to get up tomorrow and never dial your number again. If you don't want us to be together any more, I won't hold it against you; I'll understand. I'll think about the good times we've had together. Maybe I'm not the right girl for you, you should have a girl who's freer, like Karine, with a job, and . . . some other girl, anyway . . . *Beep.*'

'I'd like to hear your voice one last time, I still want to make love to you; I know it isn't going to happen again, and it hurts. You're there, I'm sure you're there, otherwise you wouldn't have suggested I come to your place . . . *Beep.*'

'I'm beginning to feel like accepting your proposal and coming to your place . . . *Beep.*'

'If you still feel like it, I think I'm going to come over . . . So pick up the phone. I don't want to come over if you have to go out . . . *Beep.*'

There aren't any words on the next message; just sniffling as Laura starts to cry. Then, mixed with her sobs: 'Hello,

hello, helloooo . . . Answer me, I'm begging you, we've got to do something . . . We could make it, you and me, we can't just let everything go like this, we can't, we just can't . . . I need to love you, you can't leave me alone tonight, you can't . . . Tell me that we'll get together tomorrow and that everything will be fine. I don't want to sacrifice my love. We'll never leave each other, we'll always be together. Even if we don't see each other much, even if we're far apart, we'll always be together. My life is fucked to pieces without you. Don't leave me wanting to die. I know we can do something else. Don't leave me without answering. Have you changed your mind? Where have you gone? Aren't you there any more? . . . He doesn't want to answer! . . . *Beep.*'

I hear shouts in the streets. I stop the answering machine and walk to the window. I see the three skinheads in camouflage pants surrounding an old Arab, as drunk as a skunk, leaning against the light green wall next to the door to the little bar. A fourth guy is with the three skins; I can't believe my eyes, it's Sammy. He's cursing the Arab along with the others. One of the guys pulls a knife from his pants pocket; the blade flicks open. Grabbing the Arab by the lapel and shaking him, he brings the blade close to his face. The Arab's head bangs against a sign that reads, 'Furnished rooms, gas and electricity'. The guy slides the knife down the Arab's chest to his crotch. I open the window and hear him say, 'You fucking Arab, I'm gonna cut your balls off and make you eat them. Isn't that what you did to the French at Sidi bel Abbès?' The old man is paralyzed; fear has made him stone-cold sober. 'No, no . . .' he repeats. The other skins are laughing. Sammy speaks to the one with the knife, to calm him down. 'Let the fucking old sand nigger be; we've got better things to do, haven't we?' The owner of the café comes out, says a few words in Arabic to the old guy. The skin closes his knife and the old guy steps into the café, walks to the back of the room and disappears.

The three skins climb on to their Harleys and start their motors. Sammy shakes their hands and hugs the one with the knife. The bikes roar off. I close the window, walk back to the answering machine, and press the playback button. Laura's voice comes on; she's calmed down, isn't crying any more:

'The last thing I wanted to tell you was that I wouldn't come to your place tonight because even if we were still together, I wouldn't have the right to. And another thing, I wish that now, at this very moment, you were on your way over to my place, and that's why you aren't answering. It would have been my big dream. All right then, goodbye! . . . Well, I won't say goodbye, just see you later . . . and I hope you're very, very happy, and I'll try to be happy without you, too . . . *Beep.*'

I call Laura, waking her up. I'm aggressive, though I don't mean to be: 'Are you out of your mind? I call to ask you to come over, and you leave me a pack of messages asking me not to abandon you. Have you gone round the bend?'

'And you're waking me at this hour just to say nasty things? Go ahead, say you don't want me any more. Say you don't love me, say we're breaking it off, that you don't want to see me any more, that you don't love me. Please say it, I need to hear you to say it, even if you don't mean it.'

'Well, fuck it, that's it! Get lost, and stop jerking me around. I never want to see or hear from you again!' I hang up. The phone rings half a minute later. I listen to Laura's first words: 'You have no right to say that! You can't just leave me like this!'

'That's enough!' I yell. I slam down the receiver, unplug the telephone, and switch off the answering machine. I take a couple of sleeping pills and go to bed.

Next morning, I go to the hospital for a blood test; I'm getting a checkup every three months these days. The virus is gradually spreading, my immune system's T-cell lymphocytes slowly dropping. But I'm lucky; I could have a more acute form of the disease.

When I come out, Laura is standing at the bottom of the hospital stairs, leaning against a stone pillar supporting the portico at the entrance. She's wearing a long navy-blue overcoat and dark glasses. It's the first sunny day of spring. I brush by her, saying, 'What the fuck are you doing here?' She follows me. 'I knew where to find you. Up until last night, you used to tell me everything you did, remember?'

I'm walking fast towards my car without looking at her. 'So?'

'So what does science have to say? That you're dying on the installment plan?'

'I'm fine, thank you.'

'Don't worry, now that I'm taking your case in hand, things will go a lot faster.'

'Meaning what?'

'Meaning you're going to pay for what you've done. I've already told you I could stop everything I was doing for you, and that I could also speed up your death. You don't want to believe me, but you're going to have to because you'll see it with your own eyes. You're going to see your body fall apart. You've fucked up my life, you've

151

given me AIDS, I'll never be able to love anyone else, so we're going to die together. Before, I was just threatening, but this time, I swear I'm going to do it.'

This sends me reeling; I feel sick. I saw stars when the nurse dug her needle into the vein at my elbow, and she had to give me a sugar cube soaked in peppermint to bring me around. This is all a bad dream, I think. But Laura says, 'Open the door for me.' Mechanically, I get into the car and open the passenger door. She sits down and says, 'Now we're going back to your place. You're going to fuck me one last time.'

'What?'

'You're going to drive me to your place and stick your cock up my belly one last time. That's all that ever worked between us, right? I don't want only to remember our bad time together at Avoriaz, when you couldn't even fuck me, you were thinking about guys so much.'

I drive, but not to my place; we head towards the other side of the 15th arrondissement. 'Where are you going?' Laura asks.

'I prefer your place. Sammy's at home.'

'Isn't he working any more?'

'Not today.'

I double-park before the gate in front of her apartment complex.

'Now get out,' I say.

'What about you?'

'I'm going home!'

'I'm not budging!'

'We'll fucking see about that!' I open the passenger door and shove her out. Laura screams, starts kicking the car; I slam the door and take off.

Sammy is still asleep when I get home. There are seven messages on the answering machine, but I don't listen to them. The phone rings; it's Laura. 'Did you listen to my messages?'

'No.'

'You should, they're very educational! All right, I'm coming over. I'm going to ring the bell, and you're going to let me in.'

'Oh, really?'

'I'll sum up what I told your answering machine: You've pushed me over the edge. You've hurt me, and I want to hurt you back, because I don't want your shit, I don't want it inside me, that's what's making me nasty. All I want is to be mean to you, to hurt you, so I'm going to screw up your health because you rejected my love. And there's another thing you should know: I know lots of the people around you, your friends, your business acquaintances, the producers who hire you. And it's so easy to make a phone call! There must be people who'd be delighted to know that you're about to die of AIDS and that you infected your girlfriend because you didn't warn her that you were HIV-positive the first time you fucked her!' I tell Laura to meet me at my place.

I go back down to the parking garage and climb into my car. As the metal garage door swings open, the white daylight from the top of the ramp hits the garage's shadowy interior, catching me directly in its glare, my eyes blinded, helpless. Maybe Laura had naïvely wanted to do me good, then, in her despair, got pain mixed up with evil. For my part, I think that only the thread of our suffering still connects me to life.

I drive on the outer boulevards, by Porte d'Aubervilliers and the Ney warehouses, very close to the rue de Crimée and the 2000 Car Park, where I used to rehearse with my old rock group, three levels down, fingers stiff with the winter cold, my body soaked with the humidity of summer. Beautiful memories of a fallen child.

I stop in front of a pay phone and call my mother. I've got a child's brain in an old man's body. I spill everything out in a rush: infecting Laura, her thinking I've rejected her love, her blackmail, her threat to tell the people around me everything; and above all, her being able to accelerate the progress of my illness, just as she has slowed it up to now. My mother can't believe her ears. 'This isn't like you, with your education and your logical mind! You don't really believe this kind of garbage, do you?' I try to tell her that it isn't a matter of believing or not believing; it's getting to me, and I'm defenseless. She tells me to come and see her.

My father is in his study, in the right wing of the house. His voice is calm, unruffled. 'At some point,' he says, 'you have to stop giving in to blackmail regardless of the consequences. I ought to know.' I think back to that night when I was eighteen. I had come home late, opened the front door to this house, and stumbled over fallen plants, overturned furniture, and smashed crockery. My mother was away in the mountains, my father and his mistress – who both had the same name, Claude – were at home, and had had a fight. My father was trying to sleep in one of the bedrooms; she was dozing on a sofa in the living room. I straightened the furniture and cleaned up the debris. She woke up and asked me to drive her to the hospital, claiming she had a broken arm. My father had trouble walking; he'd just been operated on for a torn Achilles tendon. It was four o'clock in the morning. I put the woman in my father's Renault 16, drove through empty Versailles, and dropped her off at the Richaud Hospital emergency room. She had tried everything to keep him: worked with him, called my mother, made me her ally, even told my father she had hired guys to kill him. And he'd fallen into the trap. Months, almost years passed until he decided he wouldn't give in any more. When she realized she was going to lose him, they'd had the fight.

The phone rings and my mother looks at me. It's Laura, telling her she's going to sue me for infecting her with the AIDS virus. It's a bottomless pit, like the nightmare I used to have when I was a child: no images, just the feeling of being in the center of a circle that is slowly shrinking, crushing me. 'That's fine,' my mother is telling Laura. 'Do whatever you like!'

I call my place, and Sammy answers. 'Laura just got here with a suitcase,' he says. 'She's putting her things in the closet. She says she's moving in, that it's all right with you.'

I tell him not to leave her alone in the apartment; she could tear the place up. Then I say, 'Wait for me, I'm on my way.'

I ask my father to come along; I might not have the strength to throw her out by myself. I slump in the passenger seat as he drives. We enter the apartment. I think that he may have a chance of persuading Laura, who adores him as much as she hates my mother. He starts talking to her. Sammy gets involved, grabs Laura and shoves her into the hall. My father pulls them apart, leads Laura to a corner of the living room and talks quietly to her. I'm sitting on the black sofa like a worm without any willpower. I don't say a word.

Laura repacks her suitcase. We get into my father's car and drive to the 15th arrondissement. We kiss, and she gets out. Laura looks haggard, but a small, defiant smile plays about her lips. I know it isn't over, and she knows I know. I feel like fucking her to death. She walks towards her apartment complex. As my father and I drive off, she disappears behind the fence and a small, grassy knoll.

I have dinner with my parents, pretending to be relaxed. I should stay at their place, my mother says. I refuse. I get into my car and drive back to a Paris bathed in an orange haze of lights and smog.

I push the doorbell that still has my name written under it. Laura opens the door. 'I knew you'd come,' she says. Those are practically the only words we say. Then there's just the rustle of clothes, of caresses, the dialogue of our orgasms.

I get dressed. I'm not sleeping at Laura's. Then the same endlessly repeated gestures begin again: walk to the car, open the door, start the engine, drive through the night past oncoming headlights shining like lasers.

Sammy isn't in the apartment. I turn on my desk light and take out a pen and paper. I'm writing to Laura.

'When I left your place, I drove along the bypass, and took the Porte de la Chapelle exit. I stopped at a red light. Four young people sauntered across in front of my car; two boys and two girls; they were barely twenty. I watched them walking away. At the next intersection, the light turned green. They had to run to get out of the way of the cars, so each boy grabbed a girl's hand and pulled her along. Seeing that gesture, of one hand holding another, caused me incredible pain; more than you can imagine. In a few seconds, it summed up everything you expect of me that I can't give you. Everything that you want at twenty.

'I've searched for that feeling for years, through hundreds of nights, with hundreds of bodies. I don't want you to go through that. I want you to find it: a hand holding yours, two kids in love. If it doesn't happen with me, it will happen with someone else.

'I don't want you to forget me in the way you use the word, which is drastic, absolute, and a little naïve. But I don't want to hurt you any more.

'I only ask one thing of you: if you really can help me live, by whatever method, do it, because I'm frightened and I don't deserve to die. Not like this.

'I kiss you with all my strength.'

*   *   *

As I walk through Paris, I find myself thinking that this is the only city I know where I can't lift my eyes to see what's around me. I'd like to be more observant, more responsive, but my gaze remains level or downcast, barely registering the gray of the pavements. Sometimes it swings sideways, to follow a face or a body moving away, and then it all begins again.

For certain looks, certain gestures, even if I know their sincerity will only last a few seconds, I'd wait a hundred years. Just as for all the rest of humanity, the absurdity of my actions becomes meaningful only because I'm so deeply convinced of my immortality. But I also know that my days are numbered, more than others'.

I have dinner with Marc, and we share our weariness, the things that didn't turn out for us. Our friendship is proof against time; sixteen years. He tells me about the new

157

record he's making. Maria has left him; girls are parading through his bed.

*   *   *

I leave for Africa, but it's another escape. I'm going to shoot a documentary in Abidjan and am taking Sammy along as my assistant. The producer and the director are travelling with us. We have a three-hour stopover in Madrid to change planes. Through half-closed eyes, I recognize a handsome face and a body that moves with a speedy, slightly stiff gait: Eric. He's walking between the rows of purple plastic chairs, unaware of me. He hasn't changed since that night we broke up in the glare of the riverboat spotlights. He's still a guided missile targeted at success. I call to him and we hug. Eric reproaches me for never calling him or answering the messages he's left. There's love in his look and his gestures, as if we had never split up, as if time had stopped, but I tell him it's too late. 'I gave you enough chances to come back.' Sammy watches with amusement.

Our orange taxi roars along the boulevard Giscard-d'Estaing towards the center of Abidjan through red lights and honking horns. The taxi drivers here are so nervous they're called 'black coffees'. In one of his songs, Alpha Blondy tells of the blood that's spilled along this highway to the plateau: 'Boulevard Giscard-d'Estaing, boulevard of death.'

We're put up at the Wafou Hotel. It's a luxurious place; the rooms are in huts on stilts above the lagoon. Sammy and I share a room with two big beds side by side.

158

I'm here to shoot a documentary on 'gnama-gnama'. It's a dance that the Abidjan punks do, a kind of choreographed kung fu like capoeira. When gangs from two neighborhoods meet, they back off and dance instead of fight.

I have a meeting with Siriki on the Cocody Hotel terrace. He's short, young, open-faced. Siriki is clever; he says little and speaks softly. He's already worked with Europeans on publicity shoots. 'I charge more than other people,' he tells the producer, 'but you can ask me for anything, and I'll get it for you.' The producer hesitates; I tell him to hire him.

Next day, Siriki has set up a meeting for me with two gang leaders from Treichville and Adjamé. We meet on neutral ground near the Wafou and arrange an encounter between the gangs three days later, at the Treichville bus terminal. They'll dance the gnama-gnama, and I'll film them.

In the meantime, I shoot the city: poverty next to wealth, the corrugated-iron roofs of the shanty towns below the towers of the Ivoire Hotel. I interview gang leaders, dancers, young hoods who talk 'nouchi' slang with each other. They talk about violence, about the poverty-stricken Burkina-Faso immigrants who steal to survive, and how the locals punish them by driving very long nails through their skulls and into wooden telephone poles.

It's the beginning of the rainy season, and I drive through sheets of rain in an old, very long black Datsun hired by the film production company. Sammy sits next to me; he says little, watches the dark sky.

An invisible barrier has risen between us; Sammy has

changed; maybe I have too. His work isn't as good as it used to be. I want him to learn his craft, but he seems not to care. At night, we slip between the sheets of our big twin beds, share a kiss on the cheek, sometimes just say good night. Sammy pretends not to realize that I want him, as if to tell me that he's there to work, not because he's my little stud.

The two gangs of dancers meet at the Treichville bus terminal. They parade their muscles and a whole pile of gear before my camera lens: knives, machetes, numchuks, wraparound sunglasses. Some of them are smiling but I wonder if they aren't planning to slit my throat the next minute. I speak only to the two gang leaders, Bono and Max. Siriki helps me position the dancers. I'm the only white man in the midst of these violent black bodies. I enjoy knowing that if I make the wrong move or say the wrong thing, the fragile balance could shatter and they'd tear the neighborhood apart. Terrified, the producer stays locked in the electric generator's cabin. The Treichville dancers take off their shirts; the ones from Adjamé keep theirs on. Facing each other, they get ready. I roll the camera and they dance: kicks and punches that graze opponents' cheeks without touching them, taut faces, chins held high, absolute beauty.

That evening, Sammy picks up a girl in a Treichville nightclub and we bring her back to our hut at the Wafou. I go to bed while Sammy fucks her in the living room; I can hear them moaning through the closed door. I think of Laura, of the paroxysms of our nights together and jerk off. When I go to the bathroom to wipe the sperm off my belly, I hear the girl screaming in the living room.

160

She's arguing with Sammy. I go to back to bed, but the screaming continues.

I try to sleep, but the noise keeps me awake, so I get up again, put on underwear and open the door to the living room. The girl stops yelling, but only for a moment. Sammy told her to leave, but she won't go unless he pays her more money. I calm them down. The girl claims Sammy doesn't want to pay the agreed price. Sammy says he already has, but she wants more. She starts to scream again, picks up a glass from the coffee table and crushes it in her hand. When she opens her fist, shards of glass fall on the floor, her blood drips on the carpet. Now I start yelling, 'That's enough!' I get a two-hundred-franc note and hand it to her. When the girl takes it, her blood stains the paper. I open the hut door and say, 'Get out, you lunatic!' I grab the girl by the shoulders and shove her out on to the veranda.

I slam the door, walk past Sammy and say, 'You're an asshole, you know that? Was she a good fuck, at least?'

'A real pro!'

'Did you put on a condom?'

'No.'

'Well, that's fucking marvelous! Abidjan girls are a real AIDS cesspool.'

'You're one to talk!'

Sammy goes to bed. Next morning, he gets up early and packs the camera equipment for the plane trip home. We leave, taking our stolen images of the city with us. I'll have seen Abidjan through a camera viewfinder and lost a little bit more of Sammy.

I call Laura from the airport. I feel as if I'm repeating the same gestures as a year ago, when I came back from Casablanca. I tell her I'm exhausted, worn out by images, light, the virus, us. I'd like a truce, a little peace. In a calm, somewhat husky voice, she says, 'I've just found out why I love you, and how to love you.'

She also says that she has spent all of the last week with a boy from her film school; she likes him, and thinks he finds her very attractive. But just when things should go further, she sees our bodies making love and doesn't know what to do. She can't tell him she's HIV-positive, and she's afraid of infecting him.

She too wants things to be simple, for the suffering to end. But everything can't just stop. Somewhere, there's a name for that vague force that unites us, that gets us through all the breakups.

*   *   *

Sammy rarely sleeps at the apartment any more. He makes dates with me, then doesn't show up. I call Marianne; our rivalry disappeared long ago. She says Sammy usually comes home to her, but some nights she doesn't know where he is either. She tells me about her life, how she wishes her newspaper would give her some time off to write the novel she's begun.

'Sammy has changed a lot,' I say.

'He's slipping away from me too,' she answers.

I tell her that his work in Abidjan was second-rate, that his mind seemed elsewhere. 'I tried to talk to him, but it didn't do any good. On the other hand, he finally told me his father was a harki.'*

Marianne's burst of laughter interrupts me. 'What kind of bullshit is that? His father's Spanish, like his mother! Sammy's a sly one, he knew you'd go for his having an Arab father. Even made him a harki, just to lay a cast-iron guilt trip on you!'

I suggest to Marianne that the three of us have dinner some evening, just to talk, to say things straight from the heart. She tells me that a guy she doesn't like has come to get Sammy a couple of times. 'And not a faggot, for once.'

'Is his name Pierre? Tools around on a Harley with a bunch of skinhead punks?'

'Yes.'

'So Sammy hasn't told you he's interested in alchemy!'

* * *

Late that afternoon, I go out with my video camera, looking for buildings along the beltway with lighted advertising billboards. I film their large neon letters against the darkening sky. Then I enter the buildings, climb to the top floor, and find a way to get on to the roof. I shoot the city preparing for night. I lean over the edge and frame the abyss.

Then, when the time is right, I leave the peaks for the depths, the vices of cellars and parking garages.

At times, I don't need to go out; the savage nights come to me. I'm alone with my whiskey, cigarettes and cocaine;

* Harki: an Algerian who fought with the French during the Algerian war of independence. (*Tr.*)

alone with my body, its clothes, and the liquids and excrement it produces. Using ropes, leather and steel, I do to myself what the men do to me in the city's cellars.

I decide to go all the way, to see the dawn, the watery hour of death. From my window, I film the wall across the way, its dirty, dark plaster, cracked and missing in places, a few dark red bricks showing through. Not many painters have painted the dawn. I can think of Géricault, and especially Caravaggio.

And the daylight seeps in, hard and gray, quickly growing noisy with the roar of garbage trucks and deliveries to the Prisunic shop downstairs. Nobody sees me tied up this way, bruised and soiled. I don't regret much, except that the state produced by cocaine doesn't last forever, and that even if it did, I wouldn't be able to reach a total, permanent and shameless high.

*   *   *

I meet Marianne and Sammy in a restaurant on the rue de Belleville. The weather's fine, so we eat outside. Naturally, we act as if everything were easy and casual. I give up trying to talk to Sammy about how our relationship has deteriorated. I see the painted body of a zebra under green and blue neon lights: the marquee of a former movie theater converted into a concert hall.

We walk along the boulevard's median strip, where African artists are showing off paintings on cloth. One of them has created an edible sculpture. He cut up a tuna, lacquered the head, and nailed the backbone to an upright wooden box; scraps of paper are stuck here and there around it along with little pieces of cut-up tuna, ready to be cooked on a stove.

We part, and the downhill slide continues.

*   *   *

Summer brings a kind of tranquility, though it's probably just surrender. I say yes to everything, if only because the idea of saying no makes me believe that death is closer. I do what's simplest: avoid conflict.

I spend three or four nights a week with Laura, at her place or mine. She seems happy, acts as if this could go on forever. She shows me the first pages of a screenplay she wants to write, asks me what I think of it.

By dint of saying only yes, I've moved in spite of myself from head cameraman to director of videos. Theoretically, it's a step up, but now I take orders from little showbiz honchos I find contemptible.

A record producer I know asks me to meet Mimi, the singer for a former punk band. Mimi has just recorded an album, and we write the script for a video of one of his songs together.

With his tight blue jeans, combat boots, studded belt, angelic blond hair over a thug's face, Mimi knows he'd find seducing me easy. I'm indecisive, as porous as a sponge. I gradually go along with his game. Mimi does heroin, and I accompany him on his rounds of the Arab dealers of the rue Oberkampf or avenue Parmentier. I snort brown with him, lend him money to buy his smack. He occasionally pulls a fast one, giving me ground-up aspirin and keeping the heroin for himself; I don't say anything.

165

We shoot the video at the Grands Moulins de Pantin with Laura assisting and Mimi's girlfriend Elsa in the main role. Smoking is forbidden – the clouds of dust could explode at any moment. We're risking catastrophe, but the real danger is an implosion of our jealous brains. We finish shooting late at night on the third day. We're exhausted, and the ten-year-old kids who have been working as unpaid extras, crowded behind the barbed wire, are begging for hot chocolate and croissants. We part and, in my bed, I cling to Laura's body to shield myself from the dawn.

The FR3 network is underwriting part of the video's financing, so we do the editing in Lille, in a studio at their Nord-Picardie station. There's only one room free at the Carlton Hotel, and I share a bed with Mimi. I think he expects me to caress him, but I'm paralyzed with weariness.

We return to Paris with the tape of the finished video. I see Mimi fairly often, and Laura and Elsa have long phone conversations. Laura tells her I like boys; Elsa panics at the idea that I might steal Mimi from her. 'If I find out something happened between them,' she says, 'I'm packing my bags the next minute.'
    I pick Mimi up from his tiny, impeccably neat studio. Elsa has gone out. We buy smack on the rue Arthur-Groussier and snort it in the car. We walk towards la République; Paris is hot and humid. The looks we exchange and the gestures we begin to make are unmistakable. At the Gibus, a rock band doomed to failure is tearing the smoky air apart. We leave, walk some more; clouds have hidden the stars. We go up to my place and do a couple more lines of brown. I put *Let It Bleed* on the

turntable, and Mimi sings the lyrics to 'Gimme Shelter' along with Jagger: 'Love, sister, It's just a kiss away . . .' Lying on the black and white carpet, Mimi lays his head on my thighs and I stroke his face and lips. But the images that come to me are from *Gimme Shelter*, the film of the free concert at the Altamont Speedway on December 7th, 1969. First the mob drove Jefferson Airplane off the stage; then the Rolling Stones met their match for the first time when the audience didn't fall for Mick Jagger's charm; Meredith Hunter raised his gun and moved towards the stage to shoot the singer; a Hell's Angel of the security force saw him and stabbed him. It was the death of the 'peace and love' years.

I look at Mimi and say, 'Go home. Elsa is waiting for you; afterwards, it will be too late.' He gets up heavily and vanishes down the dark hallway.

Laura calls me up the next day. Elsa told her that Mimi had spent part of the night with me and that she was sure something had happened between us. I tell Laura that I could have made love to Mimi but persuaded him to go home to Elsa instead. She doesn't believe me. 'I thought I was saving you from the evil of your life, but you're vicious and perverted, and you always will be. You take people when you feel like it and throw them away afterwards. No one's going to love you if you live like that! Your life is pretty well fucked, so go on with your shitty little love affairs and the little boys you jump or who jump you from time to time. Even if you wanted guys, wanted anybody, you could stop it if you wanted to. As for me, here's what I'm going to do: I'm going to stop wanting you. And I'm going to manage; it may be hard, it may take a long time, but I'm not staying this way any more. I just hope you don't die before you see how I've changed!'

I'm drinking tea. The last words of 'Condamné à mort' sung by Marc Ogeret are hanging in the air:

> It seems an epileptic lives next door,
> The prison's lulled by a dirge for the dead,
> Sailors on the water may see ports ahead,
> But my sleepers will flee to another shore.

I hear a key in the front door. Looking up, I see Sammy, holding an old motorcycle helmet. 'I'm taking some things. I'm leaving for Normandy.'

'You have a motorcycle?'

'Look outside.'

I go into the living room, open a window, and see a Harley-Davidson parked on the pavement. 'Is that the ticket that gets you in with the alchemists?' I ask.

'She's a beauty, eh?'

'Where did you get the cash?'

'I managed.'

'I ought to point out that you haven't paid your share of the rent for the last four months.'

Sammy's expression hardens. For a second I think, 'He's got the face of a killer.'

Sammy stuffs clothes into a backpack, comes out of his bedroom, jostles me in the hall.

'When are you coming back?'

'I don't know. We're meeting at the château, and then we're going to an alchemists' congress in Belgium.' The front door slams.

I walk into Sammy's bedroom and search through his things. I find photos of the alchemists' château, others of

168

skinheads in army-surplus pants shooting at targets shaped like men and playing war games in the countryside. Among them, I recognize Pierre and one of Sammy's rugby coaches.

I also find a book called *The Brothers of Heliopolis* by Pierre Aton. Besides directions for the hermetic Great Work, it includes some truly charming notions: a renewal of the Crusades by the West against fanatical Islam; cultural and sexual segregation of the races; a war to the death against the media, communists, Freemasons and organized religion.

Sammy returns two days later, a changed man. His face has lost the arrogance that he once wore like a second skin. I ask him what he did in Belgium; he doesn't answer. He drops his backpack in his bedroom, say's he's going to sleep at Marianne's. I get the feeling that he's going to her as if he wanted to disappear between her legs, to be swallowed up by her vagina. In the hall, he pushes the button for the elevator, turns towards me and says, 'If you hear of any work abroad, let me know; I'm interested.'

*   *   *

Laura has left film school. She claims her grandparents can't pay the tuition fees any more, but I'm inclined to think she got thrown out and is afraid to tell me.

She sees Elsa often, who tells her that Mimi is the best fuck in Paris. Mimi has started shooting up again, and I wonder how he manages to get a hard-on to fuck Elsa.

Elsa tells her that Mimi caresses her, kisses her, that they walk down the street hand in hand. She can't understand why Laura stays with me, who never shows the slightest sign of tenderness. 'Once a faggot, always a faggot!' she says.

*   *   *

I agree to do a documentary in Pakistan for a TV network. I'm to go to Karachi to film the ship graveyards where freighters and tankers end up when they can no longer be operated at a profit. They're beached on the shore, where hordes of starving workers cut up the hulls with acetylene torches to salvage the steel.

Two days before the departure, I claim to be having health problems and suggest that Sammy go in my stead. I don't say it will be his first documentary as a cameraman; the producer trusts me. Sammy is out of his mind with joy. He thanks me, kissing me on both cheeks, and again becomes the tender, slightly crazy boy I remember.

*   *   *

Laura calls me from a Trouville hotel where she's staying with Elsa. 'Don't bother coming,' she says, 'we're about to leave. We'll call each other soon . . . By the way, don't kid yourself about Mimi.'

'Meaning what?'

'Does he owe you money?'

'I lent him some to buy smack.'

170

'Elsa claims he said, "I'm not going to bother paying him his money back. He's got AIDS, he'll kick off soon!"'

'You two really are a pair of first-class bitches!' I hang up. The phone rings; it's Laura. I hang up again and turn on the answering machine.

I run a bath, pace around the apartment, put on a record. Billy Idol singing 'White Wedding' fills the room. From time to time I turn up the volume on the answering machine and hear Laura's voice. 'You're ridiculous and so am I, so stop being silly and answer me; things will go badly again. You're the king and I'm just a shit. Here I'm in an apartment that's still in your name, I don't have a job, I'm out of money, my mom's crazy, my dad's probably forgotten I even exist, I'm sick, I'm going to die before ever having a chance to live, to be someone. And you've got everything you want, your little playthings, your car, your fifty thousand phone calls a day, people at your feet. I envy your being able to hang up on people and insult them. You know that even if you insult me, I'll always be there when you feel like fucking or seeing me. Actually, you don't want things to calm down at all. You enjoy all this shit. You must be getting your rocks off, thinking, "She hasn't changed; she's just as stupid, as worthless, as ugly as ever." I can just see you saying it. But as long as you keep undermining my self-confidence and throwing the past in my face, I'll never be able to change. And you're drifting away, even though you jump me once in a while. And I've been fucked up for a lot longer than that. So you've won, once again. I'm cold and I feel bad. I'm nineteen years old, and last night I wanted to drop dead. You weren't around, of course; there was only Elsa and Mimi to help me. You're never around when I need you. I need you! How loud do I have to shout it? I'm shouting, I'm yelling, just to

171

make you listen to my breath, my breathing, to make you look at me, to pay attention to my face, to my blood. I'm going down the drain. I want to die and you don't know how to live.'

Quicksand is gradually swallowing me, and I'm clutching at straws to stay afloat. I've never been able to let myself go completely, let go of everything, let myself die to be reborn somewhere else, even when I'm on drugs or in intense pain.

Leaving my answering machine to face the flood of Laura's words, I go and sit at a table in an Arab café in Barbès. A song by Farid El-Atrache is playing on the jukebox. I watch a slim young brown-skinned boy who looks both lost and amused. His hair is shaved at the sides, a little longer on top. He's wearing jeans, immaculate white sneakers and a black nylon jacket; a red backpack lies on the floor next to his chair. He's staring at me. I stand up to go and he gestures to me to come over and sit down at his table. I tell him my name. He says, 'I'm Tillio. My parents are Italian.' I smile and say, 'Begin by lying, and things will get off to a bad start!'

'OK, my name's Jamel.'

We go for a walk along the boulevard de la Chapelle, the rue Philippe de Girard, the rue Jessaint, and then la Goutte d'Or. It's been raining, and the pavement glistens. We talk in the moonlight. Jamel is seventeen, says he's just come from Le Havre; he's going to his brother's funeral in Béthune tomorrow. Hotels are too expensive; he's looking for a place to sleep. I tell him he can come to my place. He wants to show me the graffiti on the neighborhood walls. He knows all the taggers, says they're friends of his. 'Are you part of the movement?' I ask. He's as lively as a puppy.

172

'Do you know the B.Boys?' he asks.

'Sort of. I once wanted to shoot a documentary on warehouse parties.'

'You've got to do it. Incredible things are happening on the streets right now.'

Jamel does a few lines of rap.

> *I'm Jam and I rap and I keep to myself*
> *A soldier of Allah fightin' 'gainst war,*
> *I demand that the prince who's got the power,*
> *Give the street back what belongs to us.*

He shows me his brass belt buckle, with 'JAM' in big letters on it. 'That's my name in the movement.'

'But jam is something you eat!'

'It also means a crowd . . . The army of the streets!'

'What gang do you belong to?'

'I don't. I know them all, but I keep to myself. Jam the solitary rapper!'

'Do me a favor and spare me this "soldier of God" and "Allah Akbar" business, and all the rest of it!'

I sense that Jamel's in a state of total confusion, hanging on to a few fixed points to stay afloat. It's the confusion of a street kid for whom a patchwork of principles has replaced ideology: a pinch of Islam handed down by his family and hysterical imams who tell the faithful that Allah blew up the *Challenger* because he didn't want man to come too close to him; a pinch of Americanism with English names and code words, Coca-Cola, and the music of Run DMC and Public Enemy in his ears all day long; a smidgen of planetary consciousness, of non-violence and anti-racism, mixed with muggings on the express and commuter trains; writing his tag everywhere like a shout, an SOS, on the métro cars, trucks, on

173

anything that moves, that can carry it along; being an outlaw, doing what's forbidden, but desperately trying to get society to notice him; dreaming of belonging, of becoming an artist, of recording a few rap records or showing large graffiti canvases in fashionable galleries.

As the elevator climbs to my floor, Jamel takes a felt-tip marker from his jacket pocket and writes his tag, 'JAM', on the wall, in big, looping, almost illegible letters.

Jamel searches through my records, turns on the TV, switches to the M6 channel and watches videos. He has to get up early to go to Béthune. 'Don't worry,' I tell him, 'I'll give you a lift.' He's surprised, thinks I'm acting strangely. Then he's wild with joy and kisses me on the cheek. He opens a bag of brown heroin and makes two lines on the table; he snorts one through a rolled-up métro ticket and hands it to me. I do the other line. More confusion, I think to myself: Jamel doesn't drink alcohol, which is forbidden, but has no problem smoking joints and doing smack. Allah must have said it was all right.

The drug spreads through my body. We go into my bedroom. I get undressed and lie down. Jamel opens his backpack, pulls out his toiletries and a baseball bat.

'What's that for?' I ask.
'For protection. And to hunt skinheads with.'
'All alone?'
'I told you: Solitary Jam . . . the skin hunter!'

Jamel undresses. His body is slim and muscular. He lies down next to me without the slightest embarrassment. I switch off the light and we go on talking, our words vague in the bedroom's darkness, blurred by the drug. I ask him about Sharif, the dead brother he's burying tomorrow, but

174

he doesn't answer. He comes close, and I feel his soft skin against my thighs. He snuggles next to me and dozes off. I try to move away from him so I can get some sleep, but each time he clings to me tighter, as if he were having a nightmare. At last I wake him up and say, 'Leave some room for me!'

After getting up at five, we're driving on the north highway through a gray dawn, fog, and trucks roaring along like angry missiles. I didn't even listen to Laura's messages on the answering machine.

Jamel starts to talk about Sharif, says he bled to death. France, Sharif's lover, spent a long time searching for him in the streets of Béthune: at Rosa's and the other bars, at other women's houses. At dawn, she finally found him. He was naked, slumped against a freight train, his legs stretched out on the gravel roadbed, hands tied to the steel of the train, in a pool of red. She could see a large, dark wound between Sharif's legs, a mass of flesh, hairs and blood. On that Thursday at dawn, France dipped her fingers in Sharif's blood.

As Jamel talked on, I found myself thinking that I've always felt Thursday was red. When I was a child, I gave a color to each day of the week: Monday was light green, Tuesday yellow, Wednesday dark green, Thursday red, Friday light gray, Saturday dark gray and Sunday white.

I slow down for the toll booth, and Jamel stops talking. I start up again and he says, 'Do you know what they did to him? They tied him to a freight car, stripped him, stuffed his underpants in his mouth to keep him from screaming, and then they cut off his cock and his balls. He fainted from loss of blood. They pulled his underpants out of his mouth and stuffed his cock and balls in. Then they pissed on him and left. Can you believe people like that exist?' With a sick feeling, I remember what Kheira told me in front of the Laughing Boar: 'You will be followed by Arab blood, by that image of my son Mounir, with his castrated genitals in his mouth.'

Jamel loved Sharif. The two of them used to meet in Paris and go and listen to rock 'n roll bands together. They would buy smack on place de Clichy and shoot it into their veins in the bathrooms of the concert hall, high on the music pounding through the walls. Jamel enjoyed watching as Sharif's eyes would go blank and beads of sweat popped out on his forehead.

Sharif had told him about France, who was married. He gave him details of how they made love, and it used to give Jamel a hard-on.

I call Laura from a gas station.

'Where are you?' she asks.

'On the northern highway.'

'Alone?'

'Yes.'

'I'm having dinner with Marc tonight. He's picking me up at nine; maybe he'll be my new boyfriend. I'm not telling you this to make you jealous. I'm telling you because he's been alone, too, since Maria left him, and he needs to be with someone.'

Turning around, I see Jamel taking packages of cookies from the shelves and hiding them under his jacket. It makes me want to laugh.

'You have until Sunday to come back,' Laura says.

Like the plague victims of the epidemic of 1188, or the criminals condemned to death and executed at Béthune in 1818 or 1909, Sharif will be laid to rest by the Charitable Order.

Twenty-three Charitable brothers are elected every two years from among the town's leading citizens; eighteen of them are in the procession to the graveyard. They met early this morning at police headquarters; the coffin containing Sharif's body was inside, lying on a big table in a storeroom. It had been shipped from Lille the night before, where the autopsy had taken place. France had claimed the body. She had asked the provost of the Charitables, a childhood friend, to give Sharif a decent burial, since the order takes no account of the religious beliefs of the dead, or of any crimes they may have committed during their lifetime.

Six Charitable brothers lift the coffin, slide poles underneath, and bear it towards the cemetery. The others walk behind in the teeth of a freezing north wind. They cross Béthune with great pomp: black suits, white gloves and cocked hats, tall figures among the furtive shadows of this Sunday morning. We follow them, Jamel sobbing next to me.

Just this side of the cemetery entrance, some young Arabs, three policemen and Inspector Mangin join the procession. The cops pay no attention to me or Jamel. It's cold, it's early, they're sleepy, and we're part of a group that has no real identity for them. A young Arab has died, and those of his race are going to the cemetery.

The Charitables carry the coffin to the grave and the gravediggers bury it. Two employees from the funeral home place the only wreath, a big bouquet of jasmine. The woman who ordered it is standing very erect next to the rectangular pit. 'That's her,' Jamel whispers to me. 'That's France.' She's about forty, tall and slim, with long blonde hair and hard features, especially her chin. Where did she manage to find all that jasmine? She nearly got it right; it's in Tunisia that boys slip a sprig of jasmine behind their ears in the evening. Sharif was Algerian; he was twenty years old.

A ray of sunshine cuts through the fog. Closing my eyes, I can see France sitting on the edge of a bed at the Départ Hotel. Sharif is standing naked in front of her, his ass tight, his whole body stretched towards France whose lips are sliding along his cock. The lighted hotel sign winks on and France pulls her mouth away from Sharif's penis; eyes lowered, she waits in silence, then says, almost laughing, 'You've got the most beautiful cock in the world!' Laura had told me practically the same thing: 'When you find a guy with a cock like yours, you hang on to him. You have the most beautiful cock in the world!' So there were two of us with the most beautiful cock in the world, and I seriously doubt we were the only ones! After making love, a sweating Sharif looks out of the window at the gathering darkness, his breath misting the pane. In Paris, I had stood before the same gathering night feeling empty, old and worn out. I'm waiting. But for what? To meet Jamel? To leave Laura? To be destroyed by a virus?

I open my eyes: Sharif and his cock are dead, a gift to the earth. We walk towards the cemetery exit. France goes over to stand in front of Mangin. 'You could at least pretend to look for whoever killed him, inspector!' she says, and walks on. I put my arm around Jamel and we follow her.

We walk through the town square, skirting the belfry; I look up at its spire rising into the white sky. France turns onto the rue du Carillon to go and open her clothing store; a salesgirl joins her. We hesitate, then go in. Our eyes meet; she sees Jamel next to me, and the way I look at him. I get the feeling she knows all about radiant bodies. 'I'm Sharif's brother,' Jamel says.

We walk to France's other shop, the Frip'Mod on the boulevard Victor-Hugo. Jamel is shivering with cold. On the rue du Carillon, France sells expensive clothes to middle-class women; at the Frip'Mod, young people come to buy American army-surplus clothes, jeans, sweat pants and leather jackets. She enjoys watching them try on the clothes. 'This is where I met Sharif,' she says. 'He came in to buy some jeans.' Jamel is still shivering. 'I'll buy you a sweater,' I say.

Jamel looks at his reflection in the full-length mirror. 'It suits you,' France says. 'Take it.' Jamel pulls the sweater up over his head; it snags his T-shirt and pulls it up as well, baring his chest. The impact of his body hits France full in the face: his brown skin, his chest like Sharif's but slimmer, a little longer. A tear runs down her cheek; France brushes it away with a small, quick gesture, but I saw the tear and so did Jamel, through the stitches of the sweater he's taking off. I want to pay for it, but France refuses. She wants to talk, asks us to stay in Béthune this evening.

We go to France's house. Her husband François Beck is a doctor, and is out on call. Jamel quickly glances around, looking for anything small and valuable that he can pocket when he leaves. 'I'm going to tell François

179

everything tonight,' she says. What does she mean by 'everything'? What doesn't François Beck already know? She comes close, draws me away from Jamel. 'We're different after they leave, aren't we?' she says. I'm having trouble understanding this woman. 'I suppose so,' I say. Jamel has disappeared; I'm afraid he's stuffing his pockets. 'I was going to meet him that Wednesday,' France continues. 'I closed the shop, but he didn't come. I waited for him, feeling the time weighing on me, you know? I was frightened, I could feel demons around me, ready to fight. There were hot, red and white demons, against pale blue demons from the north . . .' The slam of a door interrupts her.

François Beck comes into the room with Jamel in tow, holding a scalpel he's taken from one of the surgery's cabinets. 'France,' Beck says, 'you disgust me.'

Can a bedouin like Jamel ever find peace? Driven by a constant need for movement, he knows he'll wind up an abandoned body, deserted, bleeding to death like Sharif. He slits the smooth surface of his forearm with the scalpel, cutting a furrow that immediately fills with blood. A few drops fall to the tan carpet, and I think of Sammy scarring his body in front of Karine and me.

Jamel and Sammy meet in that blood. 'What date was your brother killed?' I ask. Jamel tells me the date: Wednesday night, two weeks earlier. Sammy was with the alchemists that day. He had joined them at the brotherhood's château on the coast near Dieppe. They were to ride their motorcycles to Antwerp to meet other so-called alchemists, meaning other right-wing splinter groups. They could have gone to Belgium by way of Béthune, and tortured Sharif. Sammy – a witness to, and perhaps a participant in, the killing. Was it an accident that he had returned from Antwerp changed, less arrogant, wanting to go and work abroad?

I can't get the image out of my mind: Sammy and the brothers of Heliopolis beating Sharif, tying him to the freight train, cutting off his genitals and watching him bleed to death.

Jamel the bedouin must be thinking of hot air, full of dry dust. Here in the north, there's nothing but cold and damp, spreading like the poison in my body. I tell France I have to make a phone call; I dial Laura's number, and her voice reassures me.

*   *   *

We're back in Paris. I've given Jamel a spare set of keys to my apartment. He's roaming the streets, looking for something to steal. I'm driving to the Porte de Sèvres, where Laura is waiting.

We make love. She is at peace. Sammy is far away. She thinks I'm beaten, that I've stopped thinking about boys, that she's won at last.

When I leave her to go back to my place next morning, it starts to rain. I take the mail from my box; there's a letter from Pakistan, but I don't open it. Jamel is still asleep; I get undressed and lie down next to him. He mumbles something and snuggles against me. If Laura calls tonight, I'm not going to answer.

Jamel is talking to me. He talks about Le Havre, his

181

family, being beaten, being abused, the foster homes, running away, rebellion, the suspended prison sentence.

He sees a picture of Sammy, asks who he is. Instantly, I get the image of Sharif dying, surrounded by the brothers of Heliopolis, with Sammy among them. 'He's a friend,' I say. 'He's in Pakistan.'

In his letter, Sammy writes about everything except us. Not a word about the fascist alchemists, either. He says he's been filming men with acetylene torches cutting up the hulls of beached freighters. The ships roar towards land at full power and beach close to the shore. Then legions of scrap-seekers swarm over them at low tide. The workers found an amnesiac who doesn't talk, won't even say his name, stowed away in the laundry room of a tanker. Sammy has a girlfriend named Indira. He's living at her place, but is sick of her wanting him to take her to Paris; he only fucks her in the morning, almost by reflex.

Laura calls me, but only to say that she's leaving to spend a few days with her grandparents; the answering machine takes the message. I spend the next four days with Jamel. I don't answer the phone, cancel all my appointments. He talks to me and can't understand why I'm interested in what he has to say. He gives me moments of peace. He tells me things he's never told anyone else; his words reveal sorrows without end. Hidden in a corner of the apartment, I cry; I'm crying at the minute absurdities of Jamel's fate.

Jamel leaves after the fifth night, saying, 'I need to spread my wings.' Five nights, four days, spent in the white apartment as if sealed off from the city. Making the slightest move has become torture for me. Today is the hour of winter.

I should be relieved that Jamel has left. He was always hanging around, reading the newspaper aloud over my shoulder, snatching off my headphones to find out what I was listening to. I wanted him to understand my entire life in a few seconds, whereas I had had to grill him about his past, asking the same questions again and again, helping him through the nausea some memories brought on.

He's leaving, I think. I burst out sobbing, and can't stop. Jamel doesn't realize what he's done: he's given me my tears back. It's his most beautiful gift. He's headed for Le Havre; it starts with 'H', like hate. I'd like my tears to give his life a little more meaning. Why did I let him go? We could have gone for walks, spent time in the city, but as usual, I chose to say, 'I have work to do.' Have my tears and contact with Jamel's skin washed the stains from my savage nights away?

But I'm crying as much for myself as for Jamel and that cross he bears, his fate. Do I dare take my car and drive to Le Havre ahead of the train and meet him at the station? Afterwards, it will be too late; I don't know his last name or his address. Just 'Jamel, Le Havre, NFA' – no fixed abode. He's sure to lose the piece of paper I wrote my address and phone number on, or else he'll forget it in the back pocket of his jeans when he sticks them in a washing machine.

Three-thirty in the afternoon, and I'm still crying. The phone rings; it's Jamel. He's lost, somewhere near the Gare du Nord: he wasn't able to find the Saint-Lazare station.

'Your voice sounds funny,' he says. 'Did I wake you up?'

183

'No, I was working. Do you want me to come and get you?'

'Yes, please. I need you.'

Jamel is standing in front of a brasserie on the rue Lafayette, caught in the halos of my windshield; tall, thin, and jittery, jostled by the city. He climbs in and I take off. A short time later, I stop in front of the Gare du Nord, take his hands in mine.

'I was so relieved when I saw you pull up,' he says. 'Did I put you out?' I told him I had been crying, that I couldn't stop.

I'm driving slowly. 'You know,' he murmurs, 'this isn't easy to say, but this is . . . this is the first time that anyone's cried for me . . . Well, I know you weren't just crying for me, you were crying for yourself too, for both of us . . . But still, it's the first time.'

*   *   *

Jamel is at Le Havre; Laura's in Paris. Sammy has returned from Karachi; he called in to get his things but left his bed. Marianne has moved; she's living in Montmartre, and Sammy has gone back to live with her.

I have an appointment at the Tarnier Hospital. Three doctors are standing behind a little formica table with my medical records, discussing the changes in my blood chemistry. I now have three more purple blotches on my right arm, and my T4 lymphocytes have fallen to 218/mm3. They decide to prescribe AZT: twelve tablets a day, two every four hours. At night, I'm supposed to wake up to take them.

The first days, I'm sick as a dog; I'm nauseated, my kidneys and muscles hurt, I feel both anxious and apathetic. I gradually get over it, but I can't handle drugs or alcohol any more. I give up doing cocaine.

Jamel calls me up. He's in Paris, wants to come to my place. Last night, he slept with a faggot who picked him up on the place des Innocents. In the morning, as he was leaving, he threatened the guy, frightening him into handing over some money, a leather jacket, a Walkman, and some cassettes.

Jamel shows up with a young guy from Le Havre. 'I met him on place Clichy,' he says. The guy has bleached blond hair sticking straight up on his head. We sit down at the round black table. From his pocket, the blond guy takes out a gun and his heroin works: insulin syringe, lemon, spoon, cotton-wool, a bag of brown. I take the gun, a Glock, and aim it at an announcer flickering on the TV screen. My hand doesn't shake.

Jamel and the blond share the same syringe, then offer it to me. I refuse. I go into my bedroom. Jamel follows me.

'I thought you never shot up.' I say.

'It's nothing, just a little hit from time to time.'

'I want your little blond friend to take his smack and his gun somewhere else.'

The bleached blond is gone. Laura calls; I tell her I have company and can't see her tonight. She hangs up in mid-sentence without saying goodbye. Jamel lies down beside me. We both have hard-ons but don't make love. We go to sleep.

The buzzer wakes me up. I look at the clock; it's nine-thirty. I pick up the intercom receiver; it's a woman mail carrier with a registered letter for me. I push the black button on the door buzzer.

But instead of the woman from the post office, Laura steps out of the elevator, with Maurice on his leash. I refuse to let her in. She insists, says she wants to talk to me. I tell her to wait, and close the door. I pull on sweat pants, a jacket and sneakers; I open the door and drag Laura towards the elevator.

The sunlight is dazzling. We go into a café. Laura drinks tea, I have coffee with milk. She sets down her cup and looks at me; she's hiccuping nervously, starting to cry. 'I'm frightened,' she says. 'I went in for some tests; my immune system's in bad shape, and my T-cells are down.'

'Where did you have the tests done?'

'At my gynecologist's.'

'And the T-cell count?'

'She sent the blood sample to the Pasteur Institute.'

I don't know why, but I get the feeling Laura is lying, that she's saying words she's heard me say, or read in the newspapers. All at once she says, 'If you want to leave me, go ahead, but please don't trash me. I can't help it; I didn't choose to love you.' I run my hand through my hair and sigh. 'Things are changing,' I say. She pulls a paper package out of her bag and says, 'I even brought your guy some croissants!' I get up, bumping the table, knocking the cups over. She clings to me, but I shove her away. As I leave the café I hear her screaming, 'I hate guys! I hate them and I don't want to love anybody any more!'

I step into my bedroom. Jamel is asleep, one leg sticking out from under the quilt. I walk into the living room, look out of the window: Laura is sitting on the steps of the entrance to the apartment complex across the street; she takes a spiral notebook from her bag.

I go out to buy bread and a newspaper. Just as I'm about to enter my apartment complex, I hesitate, cross the street, and speak to Laura. 'You aren't going to spend the whole day here, are you? It's pointless.'

'I don't care, I'll wait for you.'

Jamel is up. He's bare chested, wearing blue jeans. He bends down to look at the street from under the lowered blind. 'Is that her?' he asks. 'The young girl across the road? She looks like a kid.'

'She's two years older than you.'

I imagine Laura is writing something like: 'I'm cold. I want him to come and get me. And the other one is up there, his bare body on top of his. A body, in my place. If only I could stop feeling anything, stop watching those three windows, leave . . .'

Later on, she rings the downstairs doorbell. I don't let her in, so she comes in with some other tenants. I'm waiting for her in front of the elevator door. I ask her to leave. She refuses, walks towards the apartment.

'That's enough! Open the door, we can talk inside!'

'Buzz off. I never want to see or hear from you again!'

'I'm staying next to your door until you let me in!'

I pin Laura against the door and put the key in the lock. She tries to get in through the open door. I push her back. She clings to the door jamb. I pry her fingers loose and slam the door, leaving her outside.

She starts yelling in the hall. Jamel has gotten dressed,

187

pulled on a windbreaker. He doesn't see me; he's sitting, looking at the round black table; he's struggling inwardly as if making an enormous effort not to say anything, to remove himself from the scene. Laura is kicking and pounding on the door with her fists and Maurice's leash. 'My life is shot to hell,' she yells. 'This fag gave me AIDS, I can't have any kids, and he's throwing me out. Here I am like a dog, while he's getting fucked behind this door.'

I open the door and look at Laura without moving. My neighbor from across the hall opens her door and says, 'For God's sake, make her stop! I don't care, but the others are going to call the cops. In our place, we have these scenes inside, not in the hall!' I walk over to Laura and drag her screaming towards the elevator.

Another neighbor comes out, puts his arm around Laura, and slowly walks her towards his apartment. 'Why don't you come to my apartment for a few minutes, to calm down?' Laura turns to face me: 'You bastard, you're going to let me die. You'd rather have some Arab fucking you?'

Jamel appears in the doorway and says, without shouting, 'What business is it of yours? The Arab says to beat it and go fuck yourself. He doesn't want you, can't you understand?' I tell Jamel to go into the apartment. I pull Laura free of my neighbor's grasp, drag her towards my apartment.

Jamel is in my bedroom, sitting on the edge of the bed. She walks over to him, but he says, 'Don't talk to me. I don't exist, OK?'

Laura goes to the living room and sits down on the sofa. I go back and forth between the two of them. Jamel finally comes into the living room. I ask Laura to apologize. 'What did I say?' she wants to know. Jamel is standing a little distance away. Without looking at her, he says, 'You know how to talk, you're just using the wrong words. He doesn't want you, so fuck off!'

'What about you? Do you know how to talk?'

'I know how to say what I mean.'

They're watching each other. I'm silent. Jamel gets angry. 'Why do you say things like "the Arab" or "the dirty Arab"?'

'I'm not a racist, it isn't true,' she says. 'Tell him, you bastard, say it isn't true. You're such a coward you're afraid of losing both of us. It's because of you that we're saying this shit to each other.'

It's true, I don't want to choose. 'You don't know me,' Jamel says. 'You don't know a thing about my life. Did you know I was abused when I was a kid?'

'This guy fucked me up, I've got AIDS, I won't ever be able to love anyone.'

'You'll find somebody else.'

I can't help laughing; it's a kid's trick, to get her away from me. 'Go ahead and laugh,' says Laura. 'Isn't it true that you gave me AIDS?'

'You're such a fucking liar, I can't even believe the opposite of anything you say.'

'Did you tell your boyfriend here that you're HIV-positive, or did you pull the same trick on him you pulled on me?'

Jamel answers before I do: 'I don't give a damn!' And I add, 'We don't fuck.'

'Of course you don't. And weren't you the one who first started talking about Arabs? When I called you yesterday, didn't you say, "No, I can't see you tonight, I have a little visitor?" And when I told you I felt like going to the Turkish baths, didn't you say, "Oh yeah, that's a good idea. I'll go there with my little Arab?"?'

'I didn't say it like that.'

'Makes you feel ashamed, doesn't it, to have Jamel know that you talk like a little Parisian Barbie doll?' Abruptly, Jamel stands up. 'That's not cool,' he says. 'I don't need to hear that.' And to me: 'And you aren't cool either!' He suddenly goes crazy, punches the living room door with all his might and rushes out of the apartment.

I catch up with him on the stairs. He's holding his head in his hands. 'I don't want to hear stuff like that. Nobody can do that to me.'

'She's just saying anything that comes to mind. You've got to believe me. We can't wreck what we have together.'

'Nobody's ever done what you've done for me, and nobody's ever cried for me. But this is too much. I don't want to hear what I've just heard.'

Looking at his hand, I notice that several joints are bruised and swollen. 'Does that hurt?'

'It's nothing. I'd rather have hit the door than smashed her face in. Or yours.'

We go back to the apartment to find Laura sitting next to a window and a terrified Maurice trying to escape. I take Jamel into the bathroom and give him a bandage and some iodine for his hand. Laura joins us; she wants to bandage it for him. He refuses at first, then agrees. I go into the living room and look at the hole Jamel's fist made in the door.

In the kitchen, I make some tea for Laura. She's cold, so I fetch her a sweater. As I pass Jamel, he says, 'The kid isn't nasty, just too much in love.'

I hand the sweater to Laura, who is shivering in the kitchen. 'He's nice,' she says. 'I like him.'

We decide to go out, and get into my car. I want to head

190

for the Champs-Elysées to find a bank that's open. Traffic on the river front is jammed, so I turn around and take the beltway. It's even worse, we're barely moving. Jamel gets annoyed. 'It's Saturday,' he keeps on repeating. 'I want to get smashed!'

All the banks are closed. Jamel says there's no shortage of money, it's everywhere, free for the taking. I'm hungry and buy a sandwich. When I get back to the car, Jamel is gone. 'Are you happy now?' I ask Laura. 'What did you say to him?'

'Nothing. He just took off in that direction.'

I start up slowly. 'Aren't you going to look for him?' Laura asks. 'He took that street, on the right.'

'I'll never find him. There are some things you just don't say to that kind of guy.'

'You're using him. It's disgusting.'

'You think it's disgusting to be happy for a few moments?'

'He doesn't need you. There's nothing you can do for him. Is that the only thing in your life that excites you, playing with juvenile delinquents?'

As we drive along, Laura spots Jamel. I double-park and call to him, but he keeps on walking. I catch up with him, he doesn't want to talk. When I put my hand on his shoulder, Jamel stops and says he'd love to lay one on me.

Laura gets out of the car. 'How long is this going to take? What about me?' Jamel walks towards her, says, 'Don't start up again, dammit! Leave us alone to talk!'

I talk with Jamel as we walk, but the words don't go anywhere. We pass the car again. Laura jumps out, yells, pretends to leave, then comes back. Jamel says, 'Well, it had to end some day, it may as well be now. Slip me ten francs to buy some cigarettes.'

We step into a tobacconist's. He seems calmer. 'I don't know . . . I don't know any more, leave me alone.' As he walks away, I say, 'Call me tonight.'

'No . . . I don't know.'

'Promise you'll call.'

'I can't promise, because I always keep my promises and I don't know if I'll feel like calling you.'

'Promise!'

'I won't promise, but I'll make myself call.'

Jamel is gone. I get into the car and ask Laura, 'Where can I drop you?'

'I'm going with you.'

'No, you aren't. I'm taking you home.'

'I'm not going back to my place.'

We drive along the river past the Beaugrenelle towers. I tell Laura I won't forgive her for what she did today. 'So it's finished,' she says. 'You don't want me any more.' She starts to cry, chokes, screams, stamps her foot on the floor and punches the dashboard. I don't say anything. I'd like to be able to stop all this by taking her in my arms, but I just can't. I behave as if she's play-acting – and maybe she is.

The gate in front of her apartment complex is open, so I drive up to the building. I wrestle Laura to the elevators. In tears, she collapses against the mirror at the back of the elevator. People pretend not to notice, talk to their children as if we didn't exist.

We enter the apartment. We repeat the same words, then I fall silent; she talks on and on. I say only that I want to leave. She tries to stop me, blocking my way. I don't want to hit her, so I go back into the room. She takes advantage of this to lock the front door from the inside. She walks towards me, the key in her hand.

'Take me with you.'

'No.'

She goes into the kitchen, opens the window, and dangles the keys out over the ledge. 'If you don't take me with you, I'll drop them.' I keep away from her, say nothing, then say, 'Give me those keys.' She kicks the kitchen chairs and table. A bowl full of chocolate crashes to the floor. I go and stretch out on the bed and say, 'Give me those keys. Open the door and let me go.'

I pick up a knife to unscrew the lock. 'You'll never manage, I turned the bolt.' Laura is walking around me, calmly goes into the kitchen. 'You know very well I'd never drop those keys . . .' By the time I catch on, the key-ring is lying on the ground in front of the apartment complex, seventeen stories down.

I go to look for a spare set of keys, or rather pretend to.

'There is a spare key in the apartment,' Laura says.

'Give it to me.'

'I don't know where it is. I'll have to look.'

I search for it mechanically. Laura is lying on the bed. She suddenly leaps up and overturns the big white table: typewriter, papers, pens, camera and ashtrays crash to the floor. Absently, I search for the spare key in the jumble of things on the floor. Laura tears down the curtains, unhooks frames from the wall and throws them into the middle of the floor. She's screaming; gradually she starts referring to me in the third person. She says she wants to die but doesn't want people to think she was crazy, so she starts clearing up everything she just threw on the floor.

I'm lying motionless on the bed. Laura is talking to herself. 'Mom's going to find out that he didn't want to help me . . .

193

I'm going to write a long letter . . Even up there I'll go on loving him. He let me die. I'm nothing any more . . .'

I sit up on the edge of the bed, and take out her address book. Who should I call, I wonder? One of her friends in the building?

I ring up Marc. 'You've got to help me,' I say. 'I'm at Laura's place, and things are completely out of hand.' When Laura hears this, she rushes to the phone and disconnects us. I call Marc back, explain that I'm locked in, that the keys have gone out of the window, that he has to come up, and I'll tell him what to do through the door. Laura is hitting me with a broom while I'm talking; as I fend off the blows, the broom handle breaks on my forearm. Laura gets down on all fours, tries to chew through the phone wire with her teeth.

I almost burst out laughing, but instead lose control completely for the first time. Grabbing her by the wrists, I drag her to the bed, growling like an animal. My violence terrifies her, she screams even louder, seems to be suffocating, tears at her clothes.

She calms down a bit. I try to take off her pants, which are tangled around her ankles and her shoes. She pulls back. 'Don't touch me!' I manage to pull her pants off. She stands up, tries to pick up a piece of glass to slit her wrists. When I shove her back towards the bed, her head slams into the plaster wall and she scrapes her forehead.

'There's a spare key and I know where it is, I'll get it for you.'

I call up her mother. She isn't there, so I leave a message.

'Give me the spare and get dressed. We're going out.'

'I want to tidy up first.'

'No, give me the spare at once.'

194

She goes into the kitchen, takes out the spare key from under the sideboard. I open the door. She's putting on a T-shirt and jeans.

'I'm leaving now,' I say.

'Wait for me!'

'I'm going alone.'

'No! You told me to get dressed . . . that we were going out together.'

'I changed my mind, and for once it was my turn to lie.'

I walk out. She clings to me, I push her away. I walk down the hall towards the elevators. She's screaming. I shove her harder, and my hand hits her on the lips. She takes this for the ultimate disaster and falls to her knees. I lean down, take her face in my hands and kiss her quickly on the mouth. 'I'm sorry, I didn't mean to hurt you. I'm leaving, that's all.'

She races into the apartment and slams the door. I run down two flights of stairs, climb back up and listen at her door.

I call the elevator, go down to the ground floor, and walk around outside where Laura dropped the keys. From the pathways, people are looking up towards the top of the building: Laura is at the window, screaming that she wants to die. Other windows open. I'm still looking for the keys in the grass, but can't find them. Laura sees me, yells, 'That's him, he's the one, there he is!' She leans out into space and people start to scream. I go on looking for the keys; I don't believe she'd commit suicide.

But then I slowly start to get frightened. What if she really jumped while I was bent over the ground? A guy with his wife and children shouts, 'No! Don't do it! Don't jump! Don't jump!'

I go back up to the seventeenth floor to find the neighbors crowded around her door; she's refusing to open it. The bearded violin-playing mailman spots me and says, 'Well, you've come along in the nick of time.'

I speak to her softly, 'Laura, open up . . .' I say it over and over again, for a long time. 'It's all over,' she says. 'It's all over, he wouldn't help me.'

'Laura, I can't help you if you don't open the door.'

She opens up, I step in, and close the cursed door behind me.

'What are you doing here?' she asks. 'Were you afraid? My life is shot to pieces, you've fucked me up. You're all I have, and you're leaving me. I want to die.'

I'm calm again. 'All right, jump. Go ahead and jump!' I pull her to the kitchen window. 'Go ahead, jump!'

'You didn't help me. You could have taken me with you . . .'

'I didn't want to. I don't want to end this day with you.' She suddenly leans over the ledge, out into space. I catch her by the belt. 'See, you're holding me back. Now do you believe I might really jump?'

The phone rings, I answer. Laura's mother says, 'I thought things were going better.'

'I thought so too.' I persuade Laura to talk to her.

'He's the only one who can do anything for me, and he won't.'

They start an argument very quickly. Laura presses the speaker-phone button, and I hear her mother saying, 'No, you can't live for him; you have to live for yourself.'

Laura swears at her and hangs up. 'Even her . . . Even she's letting me down.' Stretched out on the bed, I burst out laughing. 'You don't love me,' she says. 'Not even a little. Nothing. You'll never love me.'

She calls her mother again. 'I can't go on living. He's

the only one, and he won't help me. He's laughing! He's even able to laugh about all this!'

'You haven't been the same since you met that boy. Everybody says so. You're looking bad; you're sad and depressed. You have everything it takes to be a success, but you have to work, do anything, keep yourself busy, and stop thinking about him.'

'I'm trying to. But I can't even get taken on as a cashier in a department store!'

'Of course you can't! People feel straightaway that something's not right with you, so they don't trust you. That boy isn't normal, he'll never give you what you need. And you aren't strong enough to resist him; he's going to destroy you.'

'I know I'm not strong enough, but I love him. Do you know what that means? It's the first time it's ever happened to me, and it never will again.'

'Don't talk such nonsense!'

'Everybody is ditching me. My father took off, and he barely remembers making me. And since I got this apartment, even you're beginning to get rid of me.'

'I wanted you to learn how to be independent, to take care of yourself.'

'You're nothing but a stupid bitch.'

The doorbell rings; it's the super and a tall young woman with brown hair. 'Is everything OK?' he asks.

'No, not exactly.' He steps into the apartment, glances at the wreckage. He walks over to Laura and puts his hand on her shoulder. He's more tender than I am, I think. 'You mustn't get into such a state, Laura.'

'He wants to leave me.'

'These things happen; no reason to get so upset.'

He pulls me aside: 'The cops are here. What should I tell them?'

'I don't know.'

'Think they're needed?'

'No.'

'I'll tell them they can leave.'

'Tell them we're sorry to have bothered them.'

'This young woman called them; she works for the police. She lives in the wing across the way, and when she saw Laura about to jump out of the window, she called her colleagues.'

'She did the right thing.'

'All right, I'll tell them to leave.'

I see Marc standing in the doorway. He takes a few steps into the apartment, gives Laura a kiss. I tell him things are better, and he leaves.

'Get dressed, Laura, we're getting out of here.'

'I want to tidy up a little first.' She starts to pick up pieces of glass, various things. 'My beautiful ashtray!' she sobs.

'We're leaving now. Get dressed.'

The doorbell again: it's the cops. 'What's the trouble, sir?' I explain, apologize for disturbing them for nothing. They ask for my and Laura's ID, take a few notes.

'Would you like us to take you to the hospital, miss?'

'No!'

'Might be for the best.'

'Listen, if she doesn't want to go, you can't force her.'

They leave, and I close that door one last time.

We leave the apartment and go downstairs. Laura has Maurice on his leash; he looks as if he's gone mad. The front gate has been locked again, so the guard gives me the key. Laura sits down next to an embankment, crying. A couple of boys pass by; one of them, who is pushing a blue scooter, says, 'What's the matter, Laura?' I help her into the car, open the gate, and return the key to the guard.

Night has fallen. I take the outer bypass, heading south, but run into a traffic jam. I've decided to go back to my place, but I don't know if I can stand to end the evening with Laura. Suddenly, she speaks. 'Something bad is going to happen, I can feel it.' She's broken, drained; I have a headache. 'I'm taking you back to your mother's.'

'I'd like you to say if you love me, even a little bit.'

'Yes, I think I love you a little.'

'You can't imagine how good it feels to hear you say that. It's the first time you've said it.'

'I'm going to say something else, Laura. If I don't see Jamel again because of you, if he doesn't call me tonight, it will be all over between us.'

'He'll call.'

'You shouldn't have busted that up. What was happening between us was important.'

'I didn't understand; you should have told me.'

'Told you? You couldn't even stand having him around!'

'If I had known it was important to you, I never would have come this morning.'

'You're lying; it would have been worse – assuming that's possible. Sammy never gave me what Jamel gives me a dozen times a day.'

'Sammy always made fun of you; I told you so.'

'Because it suited you. With Sammy, I knew exactly what I was doing.'

'Still, he made fun of you . . . But here I give you

everything, and you throw me away. I don't get it. I'm lovable, too. Makes no sense.'

'I needed Jamel.'

'He'll call you. He needs you, too.'

I park on the rue Blomet, back up to make room for a blind man crossing the street. Laura pushes the intercom button. I'm relieved her mother is at home. Laura says she wants to spend the night with her. I fetch the dog from the car. Laura wants to buy a book from the shop across the street. She wants me to pick out a book I'd like her to read, something that comes from me. My mind's blank; I pick a book by Paul Bowles, almost at random. She pays for it.

I kiss her on the cheeks and furtively on the lips. She's walking towards the building gate, I towards my car, we wave at each other.

Traffic jams are everywhere; it takes me more than an hour to get home. A message from Jamel is waiting on the answering machine, saying he'll call back. I don't even know if I feel like seeing him. I run a bath.

The phone rings, it's Jamel, sounding very pleased with his day. 'What are you doing?' he asks. I should be shouting, telling him to come over right away, that we'll spend the evening together, but I only say, 'I don't know. What about you?' He feels like celebrating with me. He's at Saint-Michel, wants to come over.

'How will you get here?' I ask.

'Don't worry about the color of the horse.'

'But . . .'

'But what?'

'Nothing.'

'You said, "But".'

'I'll be waiting for you. How long will it take you?'

His tone becomes distant and hard. 'Can't say.' He hangs up.

The bath is full. Slowly I slip into the scalding water. I don't know if Jamel is coming. I close my eyes. I hurt for Laura.

The intercom buzzes; it's Jamel. He's in a great mood, a little drunk. 'I thought it over,' he says, 'and you're right: we mustn't wreck what we have together!' He rushes over and hugs me.

He shows me his day's booty: a leather briefcase, a pair of sunglasses, four hundred francs and a camera. He hands me the camera. 'Here, this is for you; it's a present!'

He wants me to come to a party at an abondoned chemical plant: a warehouse party with dancers, rappers, and graffiti artists. 'The big boys of the movement will be there, even guys who worked in New York. I might sing.' I tell Jamel that I can't go with him; this endless day has done me in.

'No sweat,' he says. 'I'll see you later.'

He takes his backpack and his baseball bat.

'In case the skins show up . . . They'll get a warm welcome.'

Jamel has returned to the street, I'm beyond exhaustion. I mount my camera on a tripod and film myself, naked. I jerk off in front of the lens, but my nakedness is no triumph. I feel my body going slack, giving up. It's covered with brown spots; an excess of melanin.

The phone rings. Won't this day ever end? It's Laura's

mother, begging me to come over at once. Laura is smashing everything in the apartment; she's crying, screaming, lashing out, suffocating. 'You have to come; we'll have her admitted to a hospital. She's gone crazy!'

'She went crazy a long time ago!'

The black and orange ribbon of the bypass; Porte de Versailles; the rue Blomet. I lean on the intercom button; Laura's mother lets me in. She's called the psychiatric wards of every hospital in Paris, and none of them has any room; there's a three-week waiting period for urgent cases! So she found a private clinic in Vincennes: 'A very nice place where lots of show business people go.'

Laura calms down when she sees me, but only until she realizes I'm there to take her to the clinic. She tries to hit me, but I control her. Her mother stuffs clothes into a suitcase. Suddenly, Laura becomes docile, picks up an old stuffed bear and holds it to her cheek. She follows me out to the landing. Her mother closes the door, and we get into the elevator. On the way down, Laura comes close to me, rubs her crotch against mine. 'You could make everything all right if you wanted to, if you'd only fuck me right now.' Her eyes elsewhere, her mother pretends not to hear.

We step out of the elevator, walk towards my car. Laura is still huddled against me, stroking my fly. 'Come on, take me to your place. You'll see, everything will be all right. You'll make me come . . . I want your cock; give it to me . . . Mom, you can't imagine how he made me come. I'm sure nobody's ever made you come like that!' Her mother mutters something I can't hear. I lead her towards the car, making a great effort not to say, 'Yes I'll take you to my place, and we'll come like we've never come before.'

Suddenly she bolts into the middle of the road and lies down on the pavement; a car slams on its brakes and stops six feet from her. I kneel down and pick her up, she struggles, I drag her to my car and shove her inside. She pounds on the roof and the windows. Her mother tries to control her.

Then Laura calms down again. She's like a child, her face against the bear's threadbare fur, indifferent to her fate.

The Vincennes streets are empty. I park in front of a large white wall. We go into the clinic: there's a security guard in a small pavilion, a nineteenth-century house with a garden, a more modern building further on. Laura is admitted, and we're taken to the second story of the modern building: a locked ward. We set Laura's things down in a small room and wait for the doctor on duty. In the corridor, I see zombie faces on worn-out bodies: drug addicts, attempted suicides, schizophrenics, depressives. 'My God,' I think to myself, 'I can't believe this. We aren't going to leave Laura in this hellhole?'

The doctor appears. After talking with Laura alone, he says he's moving her to the open ward on the first floor. Her mother and I exchange a relieved glance. We carry her things down to another room. The doctor talks with Laura's mother, alone, then asks to talk with me. I tell him everything: the year-and-a-half together, sex, love, fights, blackmail. I tell him I'm HIV-positive, that I may have infected her. That's what she claims, but I don't know if she's telling the truth. I ask the doctor to do a blood test without her knowledge.

I kiss Laura on the cheek; she buries her face·in my shoulder, says, 'Please don't try to leave me in order to save me.'

Driving towards the 13th arrondissement, I feel as if I've led an animal to the slaughter. I'm hungry, so I suggest to Laura's mother that we have a bite to eat in a brasserie on the avenue de la Motte-Picquet. She tells me about her past: Algeria in the old days; her father's orange groves between Oran and Tlemcen; the war; emigrating; Marseilles; meeting Laura's father, the scion of one of Spain's great republican families; the accident of Laura's birth; the divorce; making her way to Paris; becoming the mistress of a famous singer; show business; the affair she's having with the head of the ad agency where she works - and which Laura mustn't know anything about. 'The way she's been, she could wreck everything!' I pay the bill and we part.

I exit from the bypass at the Porte de Bagnolet. I don't even feel like going to bed; I'll catch up with Jamel. I head for the abandoned chemical plant where the warehouse party is under way. I try to drive down the rue David-d'Angers, but find it blocked by police buses at place Rhin-et-Danube. People are running in every direction, and the beams from ambulances' revolving lights sweep across the building façades. I turn around and head home.

I take a right at the corner of the avenue Gambetta and the rue Pelleport and meet a group of Harleys starting up. I'm almost sure I recognize Pierre Aton on one of the bikes.

I park in the underground garage, take the elevator up, and get off at the first floor. I press the hall-light timer and take out my keys, but notice that the door to the apartment is ajar. Cold sweat runs down my back. I need a weapon; I wrap the key chain in my fist, leaving one key sticking out between my fingers. I push the door open, slowly walk in.

The apartment has been completely wrecked: the

furniture overturned, wardrobe emptied, books torn, the sofa slashed. The guts of my stereo litter the floor, and my video camera is in the bathroom, covered with shit. Three words are scrawled in red on the wall: "Fag," "Arab" and "AIDS." I close the front door.

Jamel is lying on his stomach on the bathroom floor, huddled on the tiles, his clothes torn, underwear at his ankles, his ass bloody. I touch his shoulder but he pushes my hand away. 'They were looking for Sammy.' I try to find out what happened at the rue David-d'Angers, but Jamel won't say.

He gets dressed, pulls off the belt with 'JAM' written on the buckle and throws it on my bedroom floor, staggers to the front door. Just as he puts his hand on the handle, someone knocks on the door and a voice shouts, 'Police!' Jamel stops dead in his tracks, then backs away down the passage. I open the door to find three men, two with guns drawn, the third holding a piece of paper and a red backpack. He shows me the paper, on which my name and address are written. I recognize it; I wrote them down for Jamel and was afraid he'd lose the paper in Le Havre.

'This is you, right?'

'Yes.'

'Who wrote it?'

'I did.'

He shows me the backpack. 'What about this?'

'I lost it yesterday.'

The two armed cops pin me to the wall; the younger of the two lays the barrel of his gun against my temple and says, 'Just don't give us any trouble, OK?' The third steps into the living room to search the apartment. I hear him say, 'Shit, there's been a hurricane in here!'

'I had a fight with my girlfriend.' The gun barrel shifts on my temple. 'Who's the owner of this bag?' I expect them to start hitting me, but they catch sight of Jamel walking along the passage. 'Keep your shirt on,' he says. 'Here I am.' One of the cops frisks him, says, 'Give me your ID.' Jamel pulls a passport from the back pocket of his jeans: 'Abdel Kader Douadi, Algerian, illegal alien. I'll come quietly.'

'Well, aren't you a loudmouth!'

'What's he done wrong?' I ask. 'You can't just haul him off like this!'

'Think we need your permission?' The cop points at the wreckage in the living room. 'Mind your own business; looks as if you've got your work cut out for you!' They leave, slamming the door. From the window I see Jamel, his hands handcuffed behind his back, crossing the street between the two cops. He turns around, sees me and smiles, then climbs into the black and white car. The car starts, the siren and revolving light go on, I see Jamel's neck in the rear window. It's dawn, of course.

Nothing in the day's newspapers. I call Sammy and warn him that Pierre Aton is looking for him. 'They don't have Marianne's new address,' he says. 'They don't know anything about her.'

Next day, I read every article I can find about the warehouse party that ended in bloodshed. Skinheads showed up, as Jamel had expected, and a general brawl broke out, with knives, iron bars and baseball bats, and plenty of wounded on both sides. One of the B.Boys and a skinhead leader called Panik fought single-handed. The B.Boy demolished Panik with a baseball bat, leaving him on the pavement with a broken back and his legs paralyzed; he isn't expected to walk again. Nobody knows who gave Panik the beating; neither the skins nor the

B.Boys are talking. But the reporters all caught one little sentence, as if about to become the stuff of legend: 'Only Jam could have done that!'

I get Jamel's belt from my bedroom, put it in a plastic carrier, and go downstairs to my car.

It's night. I park near the Bercy bridge, walk along the embankment. I stop, look at the shapes of the men below, heading for the sex subways. I pull the belt from the carrier and throw it into the river. As it hits the water, the light from a streetlight catches the brass buckle and sends me a glint of sunlight. The water closes over Jamel's belt and the three letters, 'JAM'.

I call a friend who is an examining magistrate, and he tells me how to find out where Jamel is being held.

The Paris prefect has decided to have him deported immediately, I learn; Jamel is in a detention center near Orly airport.

In the rain, I weave between the cars on the bypass and the highway to the detention center, but Jamel has already left. I climb back into my car and rush to the airport. Looking up at the big information screens, I learn that the plane for Algiers took off ten minutes ago. Jamel is aboard. I don't think he even knows how to speak Arabic.

Laura's mother calls me. She just got the results of the blood test the clinic did on Laura. It's negative; Laura isn't carrying the AIDS virus.

With that one word, 'negative', everything changes. At

the same time, nothing changes. Laura must have been convinced she was infected and sick; perhaps, at some moments, wanted it. Since death is inevitable, it may as well be brought by someone you love, or whom you think you love.

*   *   *

Laura calls me from the clinic. She says she can't stand it any more, that she's going to get out and find me, that we'll love each other the way we used to. I'm silent, absent. Then I say that I know the test results, that she doesn't have any hold on me, that it's as if she no longer exists. She starts to cry, her words come jerkily: 'So this is it. Your mother and all the others have won. I'm getting fifty million tons of hate over the phone, I'm nailed to the ground, and you're going to love the next girl just for not being like me. You'll be crazy about her. You know what nightmares I'm having these days? They don't stop. And I deserve better; I'm beautiful, and God knows I love you.' She shouts the last sentence: 'I love you more than truth itself!' From the dangling receiver come the sounds of a struggle, then more shouts from Laura, gradually fading.

They take her to the second floor, to the locked ward.

*   *   *

I go to the drugstore and buy insulin syringes. Bare chested in front of the bathroom mirror, I repeat the same gestures a hundred times: I dig the needle into the vein at my left elbow, pull on the plunger to draw blood into the syringe, pull the needle from my vein. Then I stand holding the syringe in my hand at arm's length like a sword, threatening my reflection in the mirror as if it weren't my own body, but that of Pierre Aton or one of the brothers of Heliopolis. Between my teeth, I say, 'I'm going to shoot my rotten blood into your veins, and you're going to die slowly, like you deserve.'

*   *   *

Laura has left the clinic. Days have passed. She's called several times. I don't want to answer.

One morning, a camera crew is at my place; we're getting ready to shoot a video. The phone rings, the assistant director answers, says it's Laura. I gesture that I'm not there, and pick up the other phone. 'Who are you?' I hear Laura ask the assistant. 'Are you hot? Do you fuck him, or does he jump you?' The assistant turns beet red and hangs up. I tell him it's nothing.

Laura writes me letters: 'I've learned all this loneliness from you. For my whole life, I'll think of the tears I shed after we made love; tears of joy, feeling that intense happiness of being at the peak of pleasure with the one you love.' One letter brings dried flower petals; another comes with a blue crystal ball. 'My love, so you can see the blue of the sky or the sea as often as you like.'

In the end I answered her, of course. I said I could never

forget her lies or her blackmail. 'I'll prove I've changed,' she said, 'and you'll come back to me.' She got a job in an outfit that does radio advertising. Someone gave her a puppy, a Siberian husky: a cross between a dog and a wolf.

Every other week, I do the lighting for a TV program. I no longer go out with my little video camera to film the city. And I can't stand afternoons any more. After lunch, I lie down on my bed, paralyzed, as if I weigh a ton. At two o'clock, the feeling of anxiety starts; it peaks at five; by eight o'clock, it's almost over. I can't concentrate when I want to think or work, and find myself thinking of cocaine and the extreme states it put me in, and which I'll never enjoy again.

The doctors have cut my AZT dosage to six tablets a day; three in the morning, three at night. It isn't as hard to take. I smile, I laugh, but only on the surface, on my lips, sometimes in my eyes. There is no laughter deep in my body. Everything strikes me as banal, even my spreading purple blotches.

One morning at seven-thirty, I go into Tarnier Hospital for a blood test. I vaguely recognize the guy ahead of me, sitting on a red vinyl chair with a rubber tourniquet around his left arm and a needle in the vein inside his elbow. The man's swollen face is deformed by Kaposi's sarcoma lesions; he can barely open his eyes. When my turn comes, I sit down in the red chair and bend to read the man's name on the nurse's register. I knew him well, he used to work with my father. He was handsome and athletic, a brilliant young engineer. Pulling on his jacket in front of me, he looks like a human rag. I say only 'Hello'.

210

He clearly recognizes me, but greets me the same way, and leaves.

Sammy has left Marianne. One evening, he came into her place as usual, and said he was leaving. She was writing an article on her computer. Marianne acted as if he wasn't there, as if he hadn't said anything, just went on typing on the keyboard. He put his things in suitcases. The door slammed. Then she collapsed and cried until morning.

Sammy is living with a girl who's a TV wardrobe mistress. He calls to ask if I can recommend a lawyer. He's going to be tried in a month and is completely at a loss, doesn't know what to do. He was smashed one night and got in a car crash. The cops wanted to take him in; he cursed at them, punched them. He was taken to a holding cell in Fleury. His girlfriend paid twenty thousand francs to bail him out.

On a Saturday afternoon, I park in front of the gate where Laura lives. I'm waiting for her. I see her walking towards me with two dogs on a leash. The husky isn't a puppy any more; he's bigger than Maurice. I kiss Laura on the cheek and say, 'You're looking a lot better than the last time I saw you!'

'Things are absolutely great these days.'

We drive along the western highway. I have to stop at my parents' to pick up some mail and tell Laura to stay in the car, but she insists on coming in.

I catch my mother's look when she sees her. With incredible cowardice, I say, 'I've come with the looney tune.' My mother says, 'What's that one doing here?' I resent her for saying that, but keep quiet. My father is

211

standing a little apart, apparently indifferent. Laura looks at him with veiled tenderness. I get my mail and we leave.

I take Laura to a roadside château near Rambouillet where Mercedes and BMWs line the parking lot and adulterous bosses and their secretaries fill the dining room. People eye us with surprise, especially Laura; in her miniskirt, she looks fresh out of school, the way she did when I first met her.

We climb into a very high bed with brass fittings. Laura is on top of me, I penetrate her, close my eyes, open them again, see the ceiling partly hidden by Laura's hair, whisper to her 'It's too good!' then other things, obscene things, and she comes without stifling her screams.

Next day, we go for a walk in the gardens, around the lake. 'You know, some day I'm going to change my life,' Laura says. 'I'm going to make some money, leave Paris, and buy a house in the country and some more huskies; I'll train them as sled dogs. I hope I won't be alone.'

Maurice falls into the château's moat, starts swimming in circles, panic-stricken. I find a place where I can climb down to the water's edge and fish him out.

We leave the château. Laura caresses me as I drive. We turn into a wooded road, make love for a long time in the car, against a tree, on the mossy ground.

I stop to buy gas. Together, we step into the service-station bathroom and make love again. Laura says she can't any more, her cunt is sore. I come in my hand, almost with regret; I wish it could last another thousand years. We part in front of the gate to her building.

I remain a slave to the same nights, but I rarely have the energy to go down into the guts of the city. I switch on my Minitel* and make dates with men who tell lies about themselves. But I don't care if they're ugly or old, so long as they satisfy my vices.

A short, stocky guy about forty, dressed in leather, is waiting for me in a café on the avenue Ledru-Rollin. We go up to his place, he offers me a glass of whiskey, I find him rather likeable. We go into his bedroom, where he opens a large wicker hamper full of leather and latex gadgets, which he spreads out on the bed. 'This must have cost a fortune!'

Ledru-Rollin has me try on a few of his playthings, then asks, 'Do you want me to hang you up?' He unfolds a leather harness and slips it over my arms and legs. He has me climb on a stool, then fastens the harness ropes to two spikes in the walls of the passage. 'I hope this is going to hold!' He pushes the stool away.

Hanging there, I feel as if I'm going limp. Ledru-Rollin wants to shave my pubic hair and my armpits. Waves of heat start rising from my feet to my skull. I feel like throwing up, and start to see stars. I ask him to unhook me before I pass out. I spend a long time lying on the bed, unable to move. He tells me that it's always like this the first time, because the harness straps cut off circulation in the femoral arteries. 'Don't worry,' he says. 'I'm a doctor.'

We go down to the building's underground parking garage. I lie down in the dust and the oil and grease stains. Ledru-Rollin stands over me, pissing.

*French telephone service that gives public access to computer bulletin boards, a number of which are do-it-yourself dating services. (Tr.)

The doctors have advised me to go to the Peupliers Clinic to have my purple blotches burned off with an argon laser. While waiting my turn, I go to the bathroom and read the inscriptions on the wall. 'I really like nurses who wear G-strings or camisoles under their uniforms. They give me a hard-on as big as a bull's. So I come here to jerk off and I come like a horse.' And right underneath: 'So where are the stains?'

The dermatologist injects anaesthetic around the blotches. He puts on protective glasses, hands me a pair, and presses a foot-pedal. The laser's ray burns my skin with a dry, metallic crackling sound. He's operating on a robot.

*   *   *

I don't remember ever seeing my father kiss my mother, take her in his arms, or hold her hand. I don't remember either of them ever touching me, with either tenderness or violence. I'm not saying that such gestures never happened, only that I don't remember any.

After that deprivation, that denial of physical yearnings, I furiously exposed my own rebellious body: I put my flesh on the line, a preamble to any other contact.

So when I get to Laura's, past midnight, I know there are gestures I should make, but can't. As I cross the lawn in front of her building, loose shutters squeak and bang against the light-colored walls. I ring the bell, the dogs bark, Laura opens the door, hardly looking at me, eyes downcast. The hall light is dark blue, you can hardly see. The husky stares at me with his one brown eye, one blue. Maurice jumps on me with delight. I follow Laura as she goes back to bed.

214

But tonight, we don't make love right away. Instead, we go to the kitchen and sit at the table drinking orgeat syrup and water; the drinks glow white in the semi-darkness. We look down on the suburbs cloaked by night: the Meudon hill, Boulogne, Issy-les-Moulineaux, hundreds of tiny glimmers of white and orange light.

I'm pained by my gestures withheld, by the tenderness I can't give Laura and won't let her give me. I needed a woman; she's still a child.

She knows all that, she says, but our embraces will endure; they'll survive jealousy, the virus, my not having any future. And suddenly I admire her ability, at twenty, to give up the idea of total love and to settle for what I give her.

I reflect on the question I asked myself when I first met Laura: 'How many men have already made her come?' I was the first. It doesn't make me especially proud. It had to be.

When I'm alone jerking off, I think of her and of the mutual fantasies our embraces revealed. Laura doesn't know the most sordid details of the depths my nights bring me to, but I know she senses those savage nights are the reason I can make her come like nobody else, because they're part of me.

Later, we make love like the first time: two lovers discovering each other, surprised by their caresses.

*   *   *

I come down with chicken pox, a childhood oversight: Pasteur Hospital, IVs, the pox on my face and body

215

swabbed with blue ointment. On the same floor, emaciated men are dying of AIDS.

People call me; I have visitors. Omar shows up, nearly in tears: his youngest brother died last night. He had stolen a van, a police car chased him, he crashed into a wall. The night before, he had lost a key an Arab woman had given him to protect him. He always wore it while breaking into places, and nobody noticed him; he was invisible.

The third day, Laura comes and sits on the edge of my bed. I can feel her fear when she sees the blue stains on my face. I know she's thinking of other lesions that might yet disfigure me. She realizes I'm not invulnerable.

*   *   *

Laura has given up trying to come to my place. She says she doesn't want to cross Paris by métro, and that she can't leave her dogs alone overnight.

After a week without news of her, I call her up. She's met a boy, a twenty-two-year-old hairdresser, and is spending her evenings and nights with him. He caresses her, tells her he loves her, that she's beautiful. He does the shopping, does the dishes, walks the dogs. They take baths together. 'I'd rather not see you,' she says. 'With you in front of me, I might start doubting him.'

Laura's absence torments me, I think of it constantly. I call at the office where she works, but too late; her hairdresser has already picked her up. I call her; the phone rings on and on. There are no messages on my answering machine.

I finally reach her one Sunday morning. 'Take me to the sea,' she says.

As we drive towards Normandy, Laura watches the pavement. My questions go unanswered. All she says is, 'I didn't think you'd react like that.'

Beyond Rouen, she says with a laugh, 'You know, he fucks me like a kid, and he doesn't make me come. If I suck him off, he comes in thirty seconds!'

There aren't any free rooms in the Trouville hotels. We cross the Belges bridge. I take a room at the Normandy, and we unpack our things. I stretch out on the bed. Laura wants to go for a walk on the beach.

'I want to fuck you!' I say.

'Now?'

'Right away.'

'Oh, so you feel like fucking me!' She climbs on to the bed, and I feverishly undress her. She's lying on her back, I'm kneeling in front of her. She jerks me off through the fly of my jeans, saying 'I've been wanting this for a long time.'

I penetrate her, pressing down hard on her body. She yells, comes very quickly. Directly afterwards, she's motionless, unseeing. I say, 'I'll come later.'

'Oh, right . . .' She gets up, walks to the bathroom like an automaton. I hear water running in the bath. Laura is washing our embrace away.

We have dinner by the Trouville beach, go for an evening walk, return to the hotel. Laura paces around the room; she turns on the TV, sits in an armchair. I'm in bed, alone. I tell her to come to bed, that I desire her. 'Well I don't want to!'

She lies down. Our bodies touch. I'm in pain, I can't

bear her rejection, her lack of desire. 'It's no big deal,' she says. 'Try to get some sleep.' She turns her back to me.

I get up, pull on my underwear and jeans.

'What are you doing?' she asks.

'I'm going back to Paris.'

'Come back to bed.' Picking up my belt from the table, I knock over a glass of orange juice. 'Shit!' I throw a bottle of mineral water against the wall. Laura gets splashed, and abruptly stands up, looking at me as if I were about to kill her. 'Let's go back to Paris.'

'Calm down,' I say. 'The bottle's plastic.'

We get back into bed. I take a couple of Seconals and finally fall asleep.

We eat breakfast next to the hotel's covered swimming pool; it's like being in a greenhouse. 'Is it going to change?' I ask.

'I don't know,' she says. 'I'm very sorry, I didn't think it would be like this. But I can't be with two people at once; I never could. I thought I was in love with him, and now I can see I'm not. But I enjoy his company, and I don't want to have sex with you right now. You've told me too often that it's finished between us, that we each have to look out for ourselves. I've learned not to feel pain, to distance myself. I was available to meet someone else, and it happened. You got me used to monotony, to only seeing each other in the evening, to saying just a few words and then fucking. I don't want that any more, even though I've learned a lot with you, and I know I'm not going to find as good a lover in a hurry. I so wanted to share some laughter, some feeling. I want to build something. With you, I'm not going anywhere.'

In the warm, humid air, I feel myself going soft. This

218

must all be a terrible misunderstanding. I can imagine sunny days with Laura in a house with a garden. I cry, but without sobbing; two warm, salty streams merely trickle from my eyes.

I wish my tears were sincere.

*   *   *

I take a plane for Lisbon to scout locations for the film Louis plans to shoot in Portugal this summer; it's the first time I'll be chief cameraman on a feature film. I'm expecting something unusual to happen.

Motionless on a pavement of the Restauradores, I'm looking at my reflection in the tinted window of a café. I'm thirty years old. My body is a little heavier, my face a bit rounder; my chin has lost some of its sharpness; my neck's thicker; my hair, ruffled by the wind, isn't as soft or as shiny as it once was. I think of Brittany, of the wild Quiberon coast, of the Port-Haliguen jetty where I used to stand and watch the sea before the yacht races. At fifteen, I was the skipper of a thirty-footer. Now, I've lost my way.

It's raining. Sheltered by an awning, two lovers are kissing against a wall of faded azulejos. The boy has his back to the wall, holding the girl glued to him, belly to belly. I hope I'll see the lovers separate when I walk near them, and glimpse, as their bodies part, the boy's unmistakable desire.

But they remain welded together. At their feet, a guitar leans against a backpack; they're standing at the foot of the Alfama, in front of the military museum, ignoring the Atlantic rain that revives me. Full of ozone and harbor smells, the warm air soaks my clothes, turns cold on my skin.

I wanted my passing to make the lovers break off their embrace under the azulejos stained by the rusty dripping of a leaky gutter. But it doesn't happen. At most, the boy's look leaves the girl's face to glance darkly at me, and only for a moment.

A taxi drops me off near the Alcantara docks. I'm looking at the 25 April Suspension Bridge, but seeing carnations of the revolution stuck in rifle barrels.

I see petals a young officer has spit on the naked body of his fiancée. I see lips swollen with desire seize the flower from the steel shaft; wolf's teeth tear the petals off, and a mouth with a crooked smile blow them towards the stretched-out girl. There are no secrets between them; they look at each other without shame. The flower has replaced the enemy's blood. The excited officer leans his rifle against a wall. A carnation petal has landed at the entrance to the girl's vagina. The officer's cock pushes it inside; this is no carnation fragment that her lover's cock is pushing up inside her, she thinks, but the blood of a virgin soldier, the blood of a young African that spattered the end of the gun barrel, where the flower was stuck. She thinks of the young man's blood moving up her vagina the way her own blood flows down, and she comes as never before. She yells the way Laura yells. Her face is Laura's face.

I go up the rua das Janelas Verdes, enter the classical art museum. It's dark and cool inside. I walk through the halls, climb a wide staircase, spend a long time in front of a fifteenth-century polyptych attributed to Nuño Gonçalves showing church leaders, soldiers and gentlemen venerating Saint Vincent de Fora.

Just as I'm about to leave, I see another painting of Saint Vincent in an alcove to the right of the polyptych. The saint is leaning against a black pillar, legs crossed, the left one extended a bit, hands behind his back; his reddish-brown hair hanging down over his ears and neck, crowned by a halo shot with golden tracery.

Saint Vincent is naked, except for a loincloth that hugs his waist and molds his sex. His slim, muscular body is slightly twisted. His eyes don't seem to be looking in the same direction. His mouth is half open, his lower lip full and sensual.

The saint is violence and tenderness, vice and purity, like a gigolo on a great city's street.

Outside, everything has changed. The rain has stopped. I sit on an old wooden bench in the April 9th Garden. The sun is shining on my face. The harbor is there, down below, beyond the tramway rails and the train tracks that hug the coast towards Estoril. Then the Tagus, light green, flecked with whitecaps; the cranes, almost hiding the Cristo Rey statue erected on the far shore; smokestacks, ships' hulls. Two young guys are walking down the gangplank of a small gray freighter flying the Panamanian flag, the *Sambrine*; one of them carries a long

221

mooring line coiled around his left shoulder, bouncing against his naked chest in rhythm with his steps.

Closer to me, a green wrought-iron balustrade, its metal curlicues revealing the wharves beyond. The weather is breathtakingly beautiful. I am alive. The world isn't just something set down out there, beyond me; I belong to it, it's mine. I will probably die of AIDS, but this isn't my life any more; I am in life.

I hire a car and drive south. I spend the night near Sagres, at the Fortaleza do Beliche. The hotel is an old fortress above the sea, a few miles from Cape Saint Vincent.

I call Laura. The hairdresser isn't living with her any more. She says: 'You only have to say one thing. Just say, "I love you", and I'll come back.' I don't know how to love.

We say obscene things to each other; carried across Europe on electric wires, they reach our ears as living breaths. We masturbate and come together.

Late the next afternoon, I push my way through a crowd of shouting Dutch tourists and climb out towards the very tip of Europe: the Cape Saint Vincent lighthouse. They say that after death, the bodies of certain saints give off a very sweet smell: the odor of sanctity. I climb down to where the fortress parapet meets the lighthouse wall; it's the farthest point west one can reach. But as I near the point, a smell, ever more precise, begins to fill the air. A smell of urine that the strong wind can't blow away. The smell of savage nights.